BEACHFRONT INHERITANCE

BOOK ONE

MICHELE GILCREST

CHAPTER 1

"Clara, you have your whole life ahead of you. Live it to the fullest. I don't want you to have regrets and end up old like me, without experiencing the kind of passion and fire that comes with falling in love. You've served everyone well in your life, but it's time to think about yourself, dear. Get out there. Open up your heart and make yourself available to love again. Promise me you will," Joan whispered.

"But, Joan. How can I think about love right now? You're sick. You need me here by your side. Who else will take care of you?"

Joan held Clara by the hand.

"Every man has an appointed time. My time has come. But you are on a different path. Make me proud. Get out there and love again."

The alarm sounded and startled Clara out of her dream. She arose with ten minutes to spare before meeting Joan's niece, Olivia, upstairs. She was on the sofa, slouched over, feeling numb over her current reality. No matter how real

Clara's dreams felt, her dear friend and boss, Joan Russell, was no longer with her.

Moments later, Clara sat upstairs watching Joan's niece pace around the living room. She suspected Olivia was searching for the right words to explain her impending dismissal. One didn't have to be a genius to figure out what was about to happen. It was inevitable now that Joan was gone. Her family members were ready to claim the estate and relieve Clara of her duties. She recalled the stories Joan used to tell her about feeling alone. All she wanted was to have loved ones who actually cared, instead of calling only when they wanted something, Joan would say. Estranged family members with distant relationships was something Joan and Clara shared in common. They bonded over Clara's ten years of service as a housekeeper. But that all came to an abrupt end after Joan lost the battle with her deteriorating health. Now, it had only been two short days since Joan's passing, and Clara was gaining firsthand experience of what the family was truly like. If only they were at her bedside during her dying days when she needed them most. If only they were there to help ease the pain and anguish Joan suffered. Clara spent the last several months at Joan's bedside watching her fade away. And now, everything had come down to one predictable conversation with her niece on a dismal Sunday afternoon.

"Clara, thank you for meeting with me today. I'm sure Aunt Joan's passing has been a whirlwind for you, as it has for the rest of us."

"It has been, Olivia. I hope you know that I meant it when I said I'm ready to help with anything you need. I know this is a tough time for everyone."

"Yes, thank you, but I think everything is under control for now. I set the arrangements for her service for Friday, and my brother and his wife are flying in on Tuesday. We'll all gather to take care of some family business on Monday, and then that's it. I've even picked out a realtor to help us take care of the house."

"So soon?" Clara asked.

"Yes, I figured it would be wise to reach out to someone with in-depth knowledge of Solomons Island. You know, someone who can really highlight what the area offers while showcasing the mansion's true value."

"I see."

Clara watched Olivia as she stared toward the lighthouse that stood towering in the distance.

"Joan always raved about Solomons Island being the best place to live in southern Maryland. I think she mentioned that she and her husband used to take the boat out on Sunday afternoons to go fishing when he was living," Clara recalled.

"Yes, I'm sure they enjoyed the tranquility. It is rather peaceful out here."

Olivia returned to her pacing.

"Clara, there's no point in prolonging the purpose of our meeting. I'm sure you're already making plans by now, anyway. I know my aunt paid you a salary, besides offering living quarters here at the mansion. With the realtor coming next week, we must have this place in pristine order to make a good first impression."

"Absolutely, Olivia. I can deep clean and help pack up Joan's medical equipment if you'd like. I'm sure the realtor will give us a couple of weeks to make sure everything is just so."

"Thank you for offering. However, time isn't exactly on our side. I've already hired a company to come in and stage everything early next week. Besides, my brother and I were thinking this would be valuable time for you to make new living arrangements and perhaps arrangements for alternative employment. Your living space will need to be staged by next week as well."

"Next week?" Clara's eyes bulged.

"Yes, dear. I know it seems sudden, but as you already know, my brother and I live out of state. We simply don't have the time to fly back and forth. We have to get everything in motion while we're here. On Monday we plan on attending the reading of Aunt Joan's will, on Tuesday the staging company will be here, and on Wednesday we'll meet with the realtor to get the ball rolling."

Clara wondered how they could plan without first knowing Joan's wishes. But she thought better of it and decided not to say anything.

"I'd be happy to have my assistant write a reference letter for you. My aunt always spoke highly of you, so that won't be an issue."

"Uh, thank you. I guess I'll need to look for a job right away and a place to stay. Just to be clear. When should I be out of the house?"

"A week from today. We'll see to it that you receive your regular paycheck, plus a bonus for the inconvenience."

Clara was stunned. She could hardly believe after all her years of service that they could strip away her employment and her place to live within the blink of an eye.

"Again, I'll have my assistant write a nice letter for you. I'm sure you can find another cleaning job in no time, hun. How difficult can it be to mop the floors and do the laundry?"

If that was Olivia's way of offering words of comfort, Clara wasn't buying it. Instead, she bit her bottom lip and tried to stop her leg from shaking uncontrollably. The mere fact that Olivia called her hun was enough to make Clara's blood boil.

"How many years have you worked with Aunt Joan again?" she asked.

"Ten. Ten years, to be exact. Joan was more like family to me than my own family members. Honestly, I think that's what Joan and I shared in common. We both had family members who cared less about us and more about themselves," Clara said.

Olivia's eyebrows were tightly knit together as she stared at Clara with her arms folded.

"Joan was one of a kind. Very thoughtful and selfless. I'm sure you wouldn't know much about that."

"You're out of line, Clara."

"Am I? You're the one who came storming in here with immediate plans to cut me loose having no regard for anyone but yourself," Clara said as she tried her best to control her trembling knees.

"I've apologized for the short notice, but there's not much else I can do. My hands are tied. The decision about how things will be arranged isn't solely up to me."

"Right." Clara fought back the tears.

"Perhaps it's best that I return to my room and start preparing for my departure. Thank you for the additional week. If you need anything, you know where to find me."

"Good evening," Olivia snarled.

Clara returned to the basement where she could be alone while she tried to wrap her mind around what just happened. She knew it wouldn't be wise to upset Olivia, seeing how she could kick her out tomorrow if she really wanted to.

As she flopped down on the sofa, Clara questioned why she hadn't prepared more carefully for her future. It was rare that a housekeeper lived in a one-bedroom basement apartment by the beach with her own private entrance. She should've known it was too good to last as long as it did. A tear trickled down her cheek.

She called her friend Mackenzie, who always had a way of making her feel better whenever she was upset.

"Hello."

"Hi, Mack. Are you busy?"

"Hey, Clara. I have about ten minutes left on my break, but I can talk. How are you?"

"I could be better." Clara sighed.

"One of those days, huh?"

"Something like it."

"Well, I guess that makes two of us. Things aren't exactly peachy over here at work."

"What's wrong?" Clara felt somewhat relieved to take her mind off her own issues for the moment.

"My boss just announced to the staff he's thinking about selling the café. He said he hasn't made a final decision yet, but why would he go as far as telling us if he wasn't seriously considering it?"

"Oh, Mack, I'm sorry. Do you think this would impact your position?"

"There's no question about it. I know I don't make a ton of money as a server, but the extra tips come in handy for me and my little girl. A one-bedroom rental costs a fortune for a single mother and her child these days. Consider yourself lucky. You really have it made living at your boss' residence."

Clara's throat tightened as she tried to take a deep breath.

"Clara, are you still there?"

"Yeah. Hold on a second. I'm just grabbing my shoes and taking a walk out back."

"You don't sound like yourself. Is everything all right?"

Clara began taking a slow stroll toward the boat slip at the back of the house. It was her quiet place where she often went to clear her mind and listen to the sound of the waves.

"Joan passed away on Friday," Clara said in a low voice.

There was silence on the other end of the line for a moment.

"Man, this really is turning out to be a rotten week, after all.

I was wondering why you didn't come by on Friday. Now I know."

Mackenzie was the only close friend Clara had in Maryland, outside of Joan. On Friday evenings Clara would go to the café, order her favorite dessert, and sit at the counter for hours with a good book. Mackenzie's curiosity got the best of her one day, and she walked right up to Clara and asked what she was reading that captured her attention for so long. The rest was history from there. The two become instant friends and the rest of the employees embraced Clara as one of their own after spending so much time there on Friday evenings.

"I know you mentioned she was pretty ill. You must be heartbroken, Clara."

"As sad as it is, I'm happy she's no longer in pain. I think Joan was sicker than she ever admitted. One would think that her niece, Olivia, would care to know more about her aunt's last days. Instead, she's already planning for a realtor to come to the house next week."

"Are you kidding me?" Mackenzie said.

"I wish I was joking, but this is no laughing matter. Her brother is arriving in a couple of days, and she's already notified me I need to be out by next Sunday."

"But that's only a week from now. What are you supposed to do? Just magically click your heels and have a new job and a new place to live overnight?"

"I know. My head is in a tailspin. The only halfway decent thing she offered was a bonus for the inconvenience. Even that felt half-hearted. She just wanted to get me out of the way so she and her greedy little brother could hurry and get their hands all over everything."

"That's awful, Clara. I wish I could offer you a place to stay. Stephanie and I barely have room in our little one bedroom. I never envisioned my little five-year-old sleeping on a pull-out couch in the living room, but it's all I can afford for now."

"Thank you, Mack. Just you being here means the world to me," Clara said.

"Are you thinking about applying for another housekeeping job?"

"More than likely. Your highness already reminded me it shouldn't be too hard. Let's see, how did she say it? 'How difficult is it to mop the floor and do the laundry?'"

"No, she didn't," Mackenzie grunted.

"Oh, yes, she did. You know, she didn't even ask questions about Joan's last days. She didn't mention one word about her. I just don't understand it."

"Don't worry, her day is coming. You can't go around treating people like that without it coming back to haunt you."

"True," Clara agreed.

"Look, why don't you come by the café around four. That's when it normally slows down on Sundays. Maybe I could whip up your favorite dessert and give you a nice hot cup of Joe while you skim the want ads. Besides, you know how delighted Josh would be to see you since you didn't come in on Friday."

"Oh, Mack, please don't start that again. Josh is a really nice guy, but I don't want him thinking there's a chance."

"Didn't Joan always say it's time you learn how to get back out there? How are you going to catch any fish if you don't extend your hook?" Mackenzie teased.

"She was right, but now is not the time. Please don't egg Josh on and make him hopeful. My head is just not in the right space."

"All right, love. Will I still see you around four?"

"Four o'clock on the dot," Clara confirmed.

"Okay, I'll see you then."

As Clara hung up the phone, she glanced toward the

mansion only to see Olivia staring from the window with a look of disdain. Making eye contact sent chills up Clara's spine. Ordinarily, she would do everything to accommodate Joan's guests. But this time, she looked away and searched for the nearest rock to toss into the water. Watching the ripple effect while trying to figure out her life would be far more productive than engaging in a staring match with the dark soul standing in the window.

CHAPTER 2

"Would you like your usual, cheesecake with black coffee? Or can I entice you to try something else?" Josh asked as he passed Clara a menu.

His section of the café was the only thing available for seating when Clara arrived. Everyone on staff knew he had a long-standing crush on her. He was the only one who still believed the crush was a secret.

She looked around before opening the menu.

"I think I'll have dinner instead."

"Well, in that case, allow me to introduce you to our crab cakes. I had a customer earlier who couldn't stop raving about them. I'm assuming you like seafood and you're not allergic."

Before Clara could answer, Mackenzie tapped Josh on the shoulder.

"Hey, Josh. I was hoping you could do me a favor and swap tables with me. Can you grab table nine while I take care of Clara? We have some catching up to do." She nodded her head, showing that he really didn't have a choice.

"But I was just telling Clara about..."

"Josh."

"Fine, she's all yours. See ya, Clara." Josh sounded defeated as he walked away.

"Poor guy. He's smitten. It's a shame you won't at least go out on one date with him. Put the poor guy out of his misery once and for all," Mackenzie said while sitting at the table.

"You and I both know that will only make matters worse. Thanks for switching tables, by the way. I didn't want to be rude, but I'm not up for a long discussion about crab cakes tonight."

"Crab cakes? You normally get dessert. He was probably so awestruck by your beauty he wasn't even thinking straight," Mackenzie teased.

"Ha ha, very funny, Mack. One of these days you're going to learn that I don't like it when people try to play matchmaker for me. It's just not my thing. Besides, I told him I want to try something for dinner tonight. I figured I can eat while I update my resume."

"All right, all right. I promised I'd stay out of it and I will. As for your job search, you know, my niece just graduated from college, and she's always talking about searching for jobs online. I can call her to see if she can recommend specific websites. In the meantime, Josh was steering you in the right direction with the crab cakes. They're to die for."

"What is it with Marylanders and crab?" Clara smiled.

"Uh, hello. We're surrounded by nothing but water filled with some of the most delicious crabs you'll ever taste. You've been here long enough to know that by now."

"You're right, but I don't know that I'll ever get used to it. I'm more of a burger and fries kind of girl. I need some comfort food now more than ever."

"I hear ya. How does a bistro burger sound? It comes on a

kaiser roll, and we can give you a little side of bistro sauce, some fries, coleslaw, you name it."

"I'll take everything you just mentioned, plus a Coke on the rocks. It looks like I may be here a while. I can't stand the thought of bumping into Olivia again, anyway. If it weren't for the fact that someone needs to feed Holly, Joan's dog, I'd never go upstairs again."

"Clara, I'm so sorry. That's no way to live. Is she staying at the house?"

"Yes, and on Tuesday her brother and his wife will be there, as well. Honestly, under normal circumstances, I don't see why the family wouldn't stay at the house. It's just Olivia's cold-hearted ways get under my skin. She's exactly as Joan described, very self-centered, just like my sister Agnes."

Clara began biting her nails without even realizing it. It was what she did when her nerves were on edge. By the looks of things, she had been doing a lot of thinking as of late and desperately needed a manicure.

"I have to believe I can land myself another housekeeping job and a place to rent in a couple of days. If not, I may have to give in and call Agnes in New York. I don't know if I can bring myself to ask her for help, Mack. If only you knew just how awful she can be." Tears welled up in Clara's eyes again.

"Clara, take a deep breath, love. It's been a long two days. You've barely had time to grieve over your loss, and now you have to deal with all this. It's a lot, but you're going to pull through it. I know you will."

Mackenzie placed her hands over Clara's.

"You're right. I can do this."

"Yes, you can. Now dry your eyes and start clicking away on that laptop of yours. I'm going to put your order in, and I'll be right back with an extra-large Coke. When I get back, we can talk, or I can help with your research. Either way, I'm here to help you figure this thing out."

"Thank you, Mack." Clara smiled and wiped her cheek.

Once Mackenzie was gone, she opened her laptop while considering her timeline. With only six days left, she was determined there had to be a position out there.

"Let's see. Start your own business in the cleaning services industry. No, that won't work. Part-time housekeeping jobs. No, I need full-time work. Five-bed, four-bath house in need of a live-in housekeeper who is hardworking, efficient, and good with pets... hmm," Clara said out loud.

"You look like you're deep in thought," Josh said as he walked up on her again.

"Hey, Josh. I'm just conducting a little research, that's all."

"Well, maybe I can help you. What are you researching?"

Clara glanced up, partially wondering why he wasn't tending to his customers' needs.

"That's kind of you, but I'm sure you're busy with customers."

"Oh, nonsense, I can spare a few minutes. Come on, show me what you're working on," he said as he peered over her shoulder.

Clara slammed her laptop shut.

"I'm good. Really, it's okay."

She immediately felt terrible for being so harsh. Any other time she'd patiently endure his random stories and inquisitiveness. But today, she didn't have it in her. With the surmounting pressure building, it was all she could do to keep a level head.

"I'm sorry. I didn't mean to be so short. I just have a lot on my mind."

"It's my fault. I have to get better at reading social cues. I'm going to let you get back to your research, but if you change your mind, you know where to find me."

"Thanks, Josh." Clara's voice trailed off.

When he was out of sight, she returned to the ad and looked up the contact information. She dialed the number and began biting her nails with each ring. Finally, voicemail came on, inviting her to leave a message at the beep.

"Good evening, I'm leaving a message regarding the housekeeping position. My name is Clara Davis, I have over ten years of experience, and I work well with pets. I'd love an opportunity to talk further, if the position is still available."

She left her number and hung up in time for Mackenzie to deliver her Coke to the table.

"Did you find a good lead?" she asked.

"I found an ad for a live-in housekeeping job. Call number one down and only forty-nine more to go before it gets late."

"Whoa, don't you think you should cut yourself some slack? You're just getting started."

"Mack, I don't have time to waste. I'm unemployed, and if I don't figure out something, I'm about to be homeless. Even if I use the small amount of funds left in my bank account, I still don't have enough to cover six months' rent. I really screwed up big time. I'm forty-eight, unemployed, single, and have the same amount of funds in my bank as I did when I was twenty-eight years old." Clara returned to biting her nails.

"Okay, we're going to work on your self-talk. If you think you're going to turn this situation around by speaking negatively about your situation, I can tell you right now it will not work. Repeat after me, 'I did not screw my life up, and I will succeed.'"

Mackenzie was big on speaking things into existence and the law of attraction, but Clara wasn't buying it. From her perspective, she got herself into this mess, and she needed to do more than speak and think positively to get herself out. Clara rolled her eyes and played along just to get her to hush.

"I did not screw up my life, and I'm going to be successful... and whatever you said."

"That last part was a little rusty, but we'll work on it. I'm going to check on table two then grab your burger, and I'll be right back. Keep practicing those positive affirmations," Mackenzie encouraged.

"Mack, if you don't mind, I think I'm going to take the burger to go. I know I came out to get away from the house, but I think I just need to focus in a quiet atmosphere. Maybe if I can sit down and get some sort of strategy in place, I can make some headway."

"Are you sure? I was looking forward to helping you. I don't get off for another two hours, but I'm more than happy to help you with the research tonight."

"I know, and I appreciate it, I really do. I just have this over-whelming feeling of wanting to be alone to sort things out."

"I understand, love. Listen, if you need anything, and I mean anything, I'm here. I'll be right back with your burger. Oh, and tomorrow I'm calling to check on you, so you better answer your phone. Understood?"

"Understood." Clara promised.

"All right, I'll be right back."

It was almost eight o'clock. Clara took her burger and emerged from the café into the warm spring air. The evenings were rather quiet on Solomons Island after everyone settled in for dinner. All that remained was the sound of an occasional passing car and the waves near the boardwalk close to the café.

Clara sat in her Honda Accord and turned over the ignition. Within ten minutes, she'd be back at the house and was looking forward to spending a quiet evening by herself. She shifted the gear in reverse but before she could see what was coming, the car was jolted, and she heard a crunching sound.

"Hey, lady, are you watching where you're going?" a man yelled from his car.

She slowly turned and looked out of her driver's window.

"Ugh, you have to be kidding me. This must be my lucky week. So much for positive affirmations," Clara mumbled.

She stepped out of the car and walked to the rear to see the damage. By then, the gentleman from the other car was walking toward her.

"Ma'am, I'm not sure how you didn't see me. I had my headlights on."

Clara looked up but was distracted by his muscular frame and the refreshing scent of his cologne. He wore a salmon-colored shirt with shorts and had a gorgeous tan.

"I saw your headlights, but I thought surely you'd wait your turn. I don't know anyone who tries to leave a parking space while the car in front of them is already moving."

"That's not exactly how it happened. Trust me, I always double check before I make my next move. I was already pulling out of my space when you put your car in reverse and just started backing up out of nowhere," he said.

"Are you trying to imply that I don't pay attention when I drive? You don't know me or my driving habits."

Clara stood there arguing adamantly, even though deep down inside, she wasn't sure if she fully checked her mirror or not. At this point, she was just mad that he was accusing her of being a terrible driver.

"Look, all I know is, I checked before pulling out of the space. Your brake lights weren't even on, so I thought it was safe to proceed," he said in a calm voice.

"Yeah, well, that still proves nothing."

"If you want proof, just look at the position of our cars. I had enough time to maneuver the car back and forth, and I was almost out of the space. But if that's not enough, I'm sure one of these shops can pull some video footage."

She held her head down, fully realizing that everything he just described about the position of the cars made sense. *What was I thinking while throwing the car in reverse? Was I really so consumed in my thoughts I wasn't even paying attention to what I was doing?*

Tears started welling up in her eyes.

"Oh, no, no. Don't do that. Don't cry. I'm sorry, ma'am. I probably sounded like a jerk with the way I walked over here just spewing off about the car. The cars can be fixed. Are you alright? I'm really sorry. I should've asked you that first."

She wiped away her tears and straightened her posture.

"It's not you. It's just been one of those days. I didn't think the day could get any worse, but this is just something else to add to the list. It's like this dark cloud is following me around wherever I go, and I can't seem to shake it, no matter how hard I try," Clara said as she started crying.

"Uh, gee, yeah, it definitely sounds like you've had a rough day."

She nodded her head in agreement.

"I have an idea. We don't need to make the day any worse by waiting for the police and filing a report. Why don't you and I just follow the honor system and come up with our own way to address the damages?"

She reached inside the car and grabbed a few tissues to pat her face dry.

"The honor system?" she asked.

"Yeah, we can exchange numbers and set a date this week to talk about how we want to handle the repairs."

"You really don't want to call the police?" she asked.

"It's just a minor fender bender. I mean, I'll need to get my headlamp fixed right away, or I could get a ticket."

"Of course. You wouldn't want that. In all likelihood you were right when you said it was my fault. My head has been in a fog today. Who knows what I was thinking when I started backing the car up."

"Hey, it happens to the best of us. If you're okay with it, how about we exchange information? My name is Mike Sanders, by the way. I'm in the area just about every day."

Clara extended her hand to introduce herself.

"Clara Covington. I don't live far from here."

She stopped to correct herself, knowing that would change in a matter of days. It occurred to Clara that she now had the added pressure of making sure his car was repaired within the next week, just in case she had to pack her bags and leave.

"Is everything all right?" he asked.

"Yes. Well, no, not really. The timing couldn't be worse. Not that you need to hear my life story, but I'm actually in the middle of trying to find a new job and a place to live. If I can't make that happen by the end of the week, I may actually have to pack my things and head back to New York. I think it would be wise to get an estimate as soon as possible, so I can write you a check for the damage. At the rate I'm going, I probably won't be a resident of Solomons Island much longer."

"Whoa, slow down there. I don't know if I can keep up. We just went from fender bender to jobless in Seattle in a matter of minutes."

Clara looked at him, not quite understanding that he was trying to make her smile.

"I'm sorry?"

"It was a joke. You know, a spinoff to the movie title Sleepless in Seattle. Get it? Jobless in Seattle. Or maybe I should've said Solomons...Jobless in Solomons? No, that doesn't sound right. Okay, maybe the joke was lame, but you get the idea."

Clara giggled.

"I appreciate you trying to make me laugh, but standup comedy isn't for everyone," she said.

"Oh, so now you're the one with jokes. Okay, I see how it is."

"You started it. Listen, all jokes aside, you're being awfully generous to make special arrangements with a lady you don't even know."

"Eh, I have a gut feeling about you. Plus, it's just a head-lamp on my part. Your bumper looks like it took more of a hit. Like I said, we can go through insurance, but I have a guy at a nearby auto body shop that can fix us right up at a fraction of the cost, and I'm sure it will save you from your insurance rates going up."

"I appreciate it. Let me write my number down on a piece of paper for you. Also, I promise to make good on my end of the bargain. My good friend works right here at the Corner Café, and I can even write the address of the place where I'll be for the next few days," Clara offered.

"I eat lunch in the Corner Café all the time. I know all the servers in there. Who's your friend?" he asked with a smile.

"Mackenzie," she said.

"Yeah, I know Mackenzie. She's one of my favorites. Don't tell the others I said so, but she makes the best malt shake in town. One time I asked Josh to make one for me, but it wasn't quite right. If you tell him I said so, I'll deny it."

Clara held up her hand and pledged 'scouts honor.'

"All right, I'm going to hold you to it. By the way, I'm not sure if you'd be interested, but there's a help wanted sign posted in the front window of the Lighthouse Tours company across the street. I heard they're looking for a front office assistant. It might be worth looking into." Mike pointed across the street.

"An office assistant? Hmm. I'm sure they'd want someone

with previous experience. I'm a housekeeper, or at least I was one. They'd probably thank me for applying and shred my resume as soon as I was out of sight."

"Well, you'll never know unless you give it a try," Mike said as he began opening his car door.

He stood with one foot in the car and pointed toward Clara.

"Don't sell yourself short. If you worked as a housekeeper, that means you're organized, pay attention to detail, and it's obvious you possess good communication skills. As for the repairs, I'll call you by the end of the day tomorrow to share the final verdict. Does that work for you?"

"Yes, that works."

"Good. Until then, check out that job opportunity. You never know what may come of it. Have yourself a good evening."

Mike waved and then got in his car. Clara watched as he finished pulling out of the parking space, then she glanced at the Lighthouse Tours place one last time, before dismissing the idea and returning to her car.

CHAPTER 3

"You have an amazing home, Mrs. Walker," Clara said as she stood in awe of her surroundings.

"Thank you, the Archer house is one of a kind. It's a historical home, originally built in the 1700s, renovated in the late seventies, and again last year. The house is over six thousand square feet, and we're looking for a new addition to our housekeeping team to help keep the place sparkling as it should."

Mrs. Walker observed Clara's appearance from head to toe while she spoke, particularly stopping to stare at her fingernails. Clara knew little about her other than she was the wife of a distinguished doctor and had a dry personality.

"Did you say that you have experience cleaning larger homes like this one?" She swung her arm around to showcase the home.

"Yes, it's the only experience I have. Although, my boss closed off a good portion of the home when her husband passed away."

Clara ran her fingers across the grain of wood on the staircase.

"Eh em. We like to make a habit of keeping our hands to ourselves at the Archer residence. There's no point in letting the hard work of the housekeeping staff go to waste by leaving fingerprints. I'm sure you can understand."

"Yes, ma'am. Sorry. I was just admiring the details in the wood."

"Please follow me to the dining room where we can sit and talk further." Mrs. Walker led the way.

At the focal point of the dining room was a crystal chandelier with what seemed like a thousand pieces dangling from above. There were windows that expanded an entire wall and invited sunlight and a gorgeous view of the Patuxent river. Clara felt a little nervous with all the fancy surroundings but was determined not to let it show.

"Ms. Covington, please, have a seat. I don't like to waste time. Interviewing isn't exactly my cup of tea. However, with selecting people who will work inside the house, it's important that I get a feel for who they really are." She crossed her leg over and leaned back.

"So...tell me about yourself. I want to know everything from your work experience to your family life and so forth."

"Okayyy." Clara paused.

It felt like this was more than your average interview, but since she desperately needed the position, Clara went along with the request.

"I don't like to beat around the bush myself, Mrs. Walker. I'm forty-eight, single, originally from New York, but I've been living here in Maryland for the last ten years."

"What brought you to Maryland, if I might ask?"

"I needed a change of scenery. My family and I aren't that close, and while I could've made a life for myself in New York, it's really expensive. Right around the time I was ready for change, I took a mini vacation to the Chesapeake Beach area, and I haven't returned since. I submitted a few applications and landed a job in Solomons Island and the rest is history."

"Deciding to live somewhere after the first visit... that's interesting. One can only imagine what you must've been running away from," Mrs. Walker said in a judgmental tone.

"Like I said, New York is fairly expensive, and my family and I aren't close. Regarding my work history, I have ten years of experience as a housekeeper. I'm not just your average run of the mill housekeeper who does a little light dusting and laundry. I have extensive experience with deep cleaning area rugs, windowsills, blinds, prepping the home for events, and more. I can even steam clean, if the proper equipment is provided."

"Name something you might typically steam clean, Ms. Covington."

"Please, call me Clara."

She glanced around the room for an example.

"These curtains of yours look like they haven't been steam cleaned in ages. I can have them looking brand new in no time."

When Clara turned back around, Mrs. Walker didn't seem too pleased with Clara's reference to the condition of her curtains.

"No offense to your current housekeeper. There's just a little technique that I picked up along the way that makes a tremendous difference," she said. Again, Mrs. Walker didn't seem too enthused.

"We usually hire a company to handle things like that." She frowned.

"Oh, I see. Well, perhaps you could save a few pennies with my services."

"Mmm, perhaps. Did you mention something about

providing references earlier? I've met with so many people I'm starting to forget who's who."

"I mentioned it on my resume. I'd be happy to provide you with a reference letter. I've also included the name and telephone number of my reference on my resume."

"That's fine. If you don't mind me asking, why are leaving your current place of employment?"

"My boss passed away."

"I'm sorry to hear it. If you were with your boss for ten years, I'm sure you had a pretty good arrangement with one another," Mrs. Walker said. It was the first time she cracked a partial smile.

"Oh, we had so much more than an arrangement. We became good friends."

"Interesting."

"This is such a small town, maybe you've heard of her. Her name was Joan Russell. Her husband was Paul Russell, although he passed away many years ago."

"The name doesn't ring a bell. I've only been here a couple of years, and my husband's work keeps us so busy socially, we don't have as much time to spend with the neighbors."

"Does your husband work nearby?" Clara asked.

"He has a position up north at Walter Reed. Solomons Island is a second home for us. It's our little getaway, which we like to regularly take advantage of whenever my husband isn't needed in Bethesda. It's important for us to have staff on hand who can keep the place up and ready for our arrival every week."

"Must be nice. I thought this was a full-time position, but it sounds like you're looking for part-time help."

"No, you read the ad correctly. It's a full-time position for the right person."

"Oh, well, in that case I hope you'll consider me."

"You and a few other candidates. I'll be making my final decision in a few days. The sooner you can provide the reference letter, the better."

Mrs. Walker stood up to escort Clara to the front door. She didn't know whether to take the abrupt ending as a negative sign or whether that was just her personality shining, rearing its ugly head.

"Thank you again for having me. I'll be sure to get the letter to you right away."

"Mmm hmm. Take care, dear."

Just like that, Clara was back in her car feeling defeated.

"Well, I guess it's back to the want ads, Bessy. Time to figure out plan B."

Bessy was the affectionate name Clara had for her car of ten years. She purchased it used right before moving to Maryland, and it had served her well ever since. Just before pulling off, she glanced at her phone and saw a few missed messages. One was from Mike, and the other was Mackenzie, calling to check on her.

"Bessy, I think it's time we make a pit stop by Lighthouse Tours. What do we have to lose?" she asked while pulling out of the driveway.

~

A chime sounded as Clara entered the storefront for Lighthouse Tours. No one was at the front desk, so she helped herself to a piece of candy and began reading the schedule posted on the wall for upcoming boat tours. She bypassed the bell on the counter to skim through a few brochures. The least she could do was brush up on basic knowledge of the business prior to asking for an interview.

"Good afternoon, may I help you?" A man's voice startled her from behind.

"Yes, my name is Clara Covington. I'm here to drop off my resume and..."

When Clara turned around, a familiar face caught her off guard.

"Mike? What are you doing here?"

"Oh, I'm just rearranging a few schedules. One of my tour guides called in sick, so I'm trying to find a replacement."

"Wait. You work here?" Clara asked.

"Yes, ma'am. I actually own the place."

"You didn't mention that last night when you were encouraging me to apply for the job."

"I didn't want you to feel pressured," he said.

Clara was intrigued by Mike and wondered why she hadn't run into him before now. Especially given that Solomons Island was a small town where mostly everyone knew each other on a first name basis. Before she could ask additional questions, the phone rang.

"Lighthouse Tours, good afternoon," he answered.

Clara continued skimming the walls, looking at fishing photos and plaques, while listening to Mike in the background.

"Yes, sir. We definitely offer fishing tours. A lot of our clients return from fishing expeditions with redfish, catfish, flounder, you name it, sir. Yes, I think I already have you down for the twentieth. Would you like for me to reschedule your tour?"

The disheveled desk, piles of paper, and the mere fact that Mike was alone was an indicator that he desperately needed help. She returned to the front desk and waited for him to hang up.

"So, did you get a quote?" Clara asked.

"A quote?"

"Yeah, for your car repairs. Your voice message said to call you back, so I just assumed it was about the price for the repairs."

"Right. I'm sorry, I've been so swamped this morning, I almost forgot. It turns out my guy won't be in the shop until tomorrow. I know that's cutting your timeline close, but I don't know anyone else out here," he said while scratching his head.

"I always go to Al's Auto Body to get my car serviced. I'm sure they'd be happy to look at your headlamp."

"Ha. Al is the guy I was referring to. When I called, they said he had a family emergency and wouldn't be back until the morning."

"That's too bad."

"Yeah, sorry about that. It's the best I can do for now."

"Hey, it's not your fault. I'll stick around and do whatever it takes to make sure your car gets repaired before I leave town."

"So, you're definitely leaving?" he asked.

"Well, nothing is definite. I went on an interview this morning, but I don't have a good feeling about it at all. And, this deadline of one week to find a job and a place to live is killing me. I just don't see how I can pull everything together under such pressure."

The phone rang again.

"Hold that thought." Mike held up his finger.

She took it upon herself to have a seat in the waiting area while he handled the call. Even if by some miracle he hired her for the assistant's job, Clara still had very little confidence in securing an apartment under such short notice. It was already Monday, and the pressure was displaying itself in the form of loss of appetite, lack of sleep, and a growing sense of hatred for Olivia. Clara dreaded the idea but wondered if she should give in and call her sister.

"Okay, sorry about that. Where were we?" he asked.

MICHELE GILCREST

"I was just rambling, really. I'm curious. How long have you been in Solomons Island? I don't recall seeing you around here before."

"That's because I've only been steady at this location for a couple of months. We have another Lighthouse Tour location in Annapolis."

"We?" Clara scrunched her eyebrows.

"Yeah, my partner Kenny and I run the business together. I used to oversee the northern tours while he ran the southern region."

"Oh, yeah, I know Kenny. Tall, slender guy. I think he's married with kids."

"Yep, that's Kenny."

"I didn't realize he had a partner. When he left, I thought maybe he sold the business to someone else. Honestly, I got so engrossed in taking care of my boss when she was sick that I lost touch with reality for a while."

"It was a quick and quiet transition. He still pops by every now and again, but his wife really wanted to be closer to her family to help out with the kids, and since I'm single it was a no brainer. Besides, I've always loved my visits to the Island, and you already know how I feel about Mackenzie's shakes."

"Yes, we can't forget about her shakes." Clara laughed.

"If you don't mind me asking, did you stop by to check in about the car, or..."

"Actually, I stopped by because I heard your voice in my head, encouraging me to come and apply for the job. I figured what did I have to lose."

"Really? I didn't think you would listen to me. I mean, I was hoping you would. Clearly, I need help."

Clara looked beyond where he was standing and then looked back at the disorganized desk.

"Clearly," she said.

"Look. I know very little about boat tours, and I certainly don't know much about technology. But if what you're looking for is someone to answer the phones, take messages, prepare a hot cup of coffee, and even help you create some sort of organized filing system, then I promise not to disappoint. I can even maintain your schedule for you. But, if you're looking for me to work with spreadsheets and fancy math, then we might have a problem."

Mike looked at Clara and smiled.

"No fancy math needed. All I need is a highly organized individual who can help me keep this place afloat, and Ms. Covington, your timing couldn't be more impeccable. I'll need to check out your references, of course. However, I'm sure Mackenzie would vouch for you. How soon can you start?"

"Wait. Are you sure about this? You sure you won't feel awkward hiring the woman you got into a car accident with?"

"Absolutely not. It was a fender bender, for goodness' sake."

"Okay, just making sure. Well, what about my professional reference? I'm happy to provide a letter for you. We should probably talk about the pay, hours, and benefits, no?"

"Whoa, slow down there. I'm happy to take any additional references that you have. As for the job details, you'll have full benefits, your hours are from eight to four, and here's the starting salary."

Mike wrote a figure on a post it note and stood back to wait for Clara's reaction.

"I can live with that. Are you sure you want to do this?"

"Do what?" he asked.

"Hire the housekeeper?"

"As long as you're sure you want the job, and you're open to learning new things."

"Yeah, I'm open. I couldn't think of a better time to try something new."

"Great, so is there any chance you can start today?"

"Today, as in right now?" she asked.

"I promise, I'm not normally this overbearing, but I'm in a pinch. I don't have anyone to run this afternoon's tour, which means I have to do it. If you could stay here and man the phones, maybe even take a few appointments, that would be awesome."

What in the world have I gotten myself into? She stood looking at her new boss. He was so easy on the eyes she was having a hard time refusing, plus she really needed the job. But she questioned if this was the wisest move. In a twenty-four-hour span, she crashed into a car while reversing out of a space, and now she's accepting a job that's completely out of her field.

"Is this for real?" she asked herself out loud.

"Yes, it's real. I'm slammed and I don't have any help," Mike said.

"Oh, no. I wasn't talking to you. Look, I appreciate the opportunity, but you caught me in the middle of a crisis. Finding the job is only half the battle. It's important, but I still need the rest of this week to find a place to live. I have to be out of my current place by Sunday. So, while I appreciate the offer, if you can't give me the time I need to get things in order, then this isn't going to work. Plus, there's Joan's funeral on Friday and come hell or high water, I plan on being there."

"Joan?" Mike looked puzzled.

"My boss. My former boss, I should say... she passed away."

"I'm sorry, I didn't realize." His voice drifted.

"No worries."

Mike came around from behind the desk and stood in front of Clara.

"It sounds like you're going through a lot. I can reach out to one of my buddies for some help. How about you take the next week to get settled, figure out your living situation, and when you're ready, we can set up a start date?"

"But what about..."

"Eh eh." Mike interrupted.

"Don't say another word. I'll worry about everything going on here while you focus on getting your life in order. I've been dealing with the chaos this long, what's another week going to do to me?"

"I don't know what to say. I've never met a generous stranger like you before."

Mike laughed.

"I've been called a lot of names in my lifetime, but that one is new. You're definitely one of a kind. Look, Clara. I think you'd make a good fit around here. There's something about your personality that's seems perfect. You seem like you can help me stay organized, and you're kind enough to be the first face everyone sees when they step into Lighthouse Tours. If it means waiting another week for you to start, I'm willing to take the chance."

"Mike, all I can say is thank you. I promise, I won't let you down."

He smiled and started heading back toward the front desk again. Clara didn't miss his cute dimples but decided from that moment on if he was going to be her new boss, she would strictly be about business and put all other thoughts about him to rest.

"I hope not. I look forward to hearing from you soon."

"Sounds good."

CHAPTER 4

*C*lara poured kibble into Holly's bowl. It was her custom to come upstairs every morning and begin the day by feeding Joan's dog. She bent down to pet Holly and envisioned what life would be like for her beyond the next few days.

Was Olivia planning to keep Holly? Did she even care to know her feeding and outdoor routines?

"Poor Holly," she said out loud.

"You might be getting an eviction notice the same way I did, sweet girl." Clara continued to pet her.

"What did you say?" Olivia asked.

Clara jumped at the sound of her voice and immediately got annoyed for always being so easily startled.

"I was just feeding Holly. I'll get out of your hair as soon as she's finished," Clara said.

"You're not bothering me. I'm glad I ran into you. I've been thinking about making arrangements for Holly to find a new home. I was wondering if you know of anyone who might be interested in taking her."

"Since you're family, I assumed that you would care for her." Clara knew better but waited for her response.

"Are you kidding me? I don't get along with anything that has four legs and fur. Aunt Joan was into animals, not me."

"Well, in that case, I'll ask around. I'm sure there's a family who's willing to take her in and give her a forever home."

"What about yourself? The two of you seem to be very fond of one another."

Clara could feel her temperature rising but took a deep breath to help her stay calm.

"Olivia, I would love nothing more than to keep Holly. However, right now I have the weight of the world on my shoulders. I need to find a place to live first before I can worry about taking in a pet. I was actually hoping that you would be gracious enough to allow me to extend my stay by a few extra days just in case-"

"I've done all I can, Clara. My brother and his family will be here this afternoon, and we have a full itinerary planned all the way through to next week. I was actually looking for you to talk about one last job that needs to be completed before your departure at the end of the week."

"And what might that be?" Clara snarled.

"Hold on, now. Let's not forget that I'm giving you a bonus check and providing a stellar reference. The least you can do is pretend to be grateful."

Clara mentally counted to ten. She was usually rather peaceful, but every bone in her body screamed for relief.

"How can I help you?" she asked.

"Now, that's more like it."

"We're expecting a minimum of thirty guests for a repast here at the house on Friday after the service. I'll need you to set up the food and take care of the arrangements. I'll see that everything is paid for. You should be in uniform and ready to prepare to serve everyone when we get back from the funeral."

"Excuse me?"

"I said you should be prepared to serve everyone. Is there a problem?" Olivia clarified.

"I don't see how I can attend Joan's funeral and be here at the same time."

"Take your pick. You need your check, don't you?"

Clara placed the dog food back on the shelf and turned to Olivia with a weary sound in her voice.

"I'll see to it that everything is ready for Friday," she said as a lump formed in her throat.

"And you'll be here to serve, correct?"

"Yes."

"Good. By the way, if you want to take the dog downstairs, that would be just fine with me. All she does is scratch at the door and whine at night."

"Come on, Holly."

Clara took Holly's water bowl and vowed to return later for the rest of her belongings. As she headed for the basement, she remained in total disbelief. In Clara's eyes, Olivia was just as cold-hearted as they come.

~

After visiting several apartments for rent Clara stopped by the café. The smell of bacon and eggs lingered in the air as she pulled out a stool at the front counter. Mack closed the cash register, refilled a customer's drink, and then slipped a menu in front of Clara.

"Is something wrong with your cell phone?" Mack asked in a sarcastic tone.

"No, I meant to call you back last night, but I fell asleep amid mapping out the apartments I wanted to visit today."

"Any luck?" Mack asked.

"There's plenty to choose from, but the rent is high enough to consume at least one of my paychecks per month."

"Paycheck? Did you get a job?"

"Yeah, I got a job working for Mike across the street at Lighthouse Tours. It has absolutely nothing to do with my experience as a housekeeper, but he was willing to hire me, so I accepted. I'm supposed to start in a week."

"You got a job working for the hottest guy in town!" Mackenzie hollered.

"Will you hush! Keep your voice down. I don't want the entire town in my business. I don't even know if I'm keeping the job yet."

"What do you mean you don't know if you're keeping it?" Mackenzie asked.

"In a perfect world where I can actually find a place to live before Sunday? Sure, why not? But if I don't, then what?"

Josh went out of his way to deliberately pass by the ladies while smiling at Clara.

"Hi, Josh." She lifted her hand without making eye contact.

"Hey, Clara,"

"What am I? Chopped liver? You can't say hello to me?" Mack protested.

"Hello, Mack." He rolled his eyes and continued walking.

Clara requested a cheesecake with a cup of coffee and slid the menu back across the counter. Mack stood with a grin on her face.

"Don't start, Mack."

"You don't know what I'm thinking."

"I bet you, I do."

"Well, you're wrong this time." She leaned in and confided.

"I think you getting a job at Lighthouse Tours is a sign," Mack suggested.

"A sign of what?"

"It's a sign of things to come. It's a fresh start, a new beginning, and if you play your cards right, you never know what else it could turn into. Come on, Clara, think about it. You remember how Joan used to always encourage you to get out there and find somebody."

"I don't hardly see the relevance." Clara sighed.

"And that, my dear, is part of your problem. You have to learn how to take a step back and look at the big picture. He's smart, a business owner, hard-working, down to earth, and he's good looking. This might be your opportunity to finally meet somebody just like Joan always hoped for."

"Mack, you've been putting in way too much overtime. I think you need some rest."

"Come on! Stop being so pessimistic," she responded.

"Mackenzie, did you miss the part where I told you I would be working for the man? As in...he's going to be my new boss. Why would I ever imagine anything other than a professional relationship?"

"Eh, boss today, husband tomorrow. You wait and see. You've got way too much beauty and charm for him to resist. I see how the men look at those curves of yours. Plus, you two would make such a cute couple."

"Mackenzie, you're too much."

"Mark my words... when he trips and falls head over heels for you, I'm going to be the first one to say I told you so. By the way, how did you find out about the job?" Mackenzie asked as she poured Clara's coffee.

"I reversed into his car and damaged his headlamp. It happened just a few feet from the café after I left the other night. He was kind enough to let me off the hook as long as I agreed to repair his light. I took him up on the offer so I wouldn't have to call the insurance company. After I explained the need to expedite things due to my job situation, he told me Lighthouse Tours was hiring. I guess the rest is history."

"Wow, and just like that he offered you a job? See, he's sweet on you already." Mack placed the cheesecake in front of Clara and continued to listen.

"Will you stop carrying on about nothing? It wasn't like that at all. He just told me they were hiring. I had no idea he was the owner until I showed up to submit my resume the next morning. He even mentioned the café and how you make the best malt shakes in town. I'm not supposed to repeat that in front of Josh, so don't say anything."

"What a sweetheart. He usually comes in a couple times a week. He sits right here at the counter and orders the same thing every single time. Sounds familiar, doesn't it? He's just like somebody else I know. Two peas in a pod, I tell ya. I'll bet it's another sign."

"Oh, Mackenzie, for goodness' sake with all the signs. Nobody pays attention to that nonsense."

"Says who?" Mackenzie rested her hand on her hip.

"Says me, now enough is enough already. On to more important things, like where I'm going to live. I'm starting to get really nervous this isn't going to work out. I almost picked up the phone and called my sister last night, but my pride got in the way. I'd almost rather be homeless than have to ask her for help."

"Do you want my advice?" Mackenzie asked.

"I'm listening."

With her mug in hand, Clara sat eager to hear what Mack had to say. She tucked her strawberry curls behind her ear while taking another sip of coffee.

"Even if it cost you one paycheck per month, go ahead and

secure a lease. You'll get pay raises in the future. What's most important now is you have a roof over your head. Going back to New York isn't the solution and you know it."

"Perhaps, but it doesn't seem wise to spend fifty percent of my pay on rent. It's bad enough that I don't have much of a savings. How will I ever get ahead?" Clara said in a somber voice.

"Clara, trust me when I tell you it won't always be this way. Focus on fixing your current situation. That way you can tell that little heifer, Olivia, to kiss you where the sun don't shine."

Clara spit coffee all over her cheesecake and tried to cover her mouth before anything else came out. Every head within a few feet of where they stood turned to see what all the fuss was about. It was a good thing Mackenzie's boss wasn't in yet. The two laughed and carried on with each other terribly when he wasn't there.

"And that's exactly what I'd like to tell her, too. Can you believe she had the audacity to ask me to stay back at the house and be ready to serve everyone who arrives after the funeral? I guess she just assumed I wasn't going. When I mentioned that I planned on attending the funeral, all she did was dangle the bonus check over my head like some sort of subtle threat."

"Don't worry, her day is coming. You just wait and see," Mack said.

"It couldn't come soon enough," Clara agreed.

"So, out of all the apartments you visited, which one was your favorite?"

"If we're looking at affordability, I'd have to leave this immediate area and head to some other part of St. Mary's county. If we're focused on a short commute and convenience, then there's several places nearby that I could call home."

"Well then, that settles it. Hold that thought, I'll be right back." Mackenzie rang up another customer who was ready to check out.

While sipping the remainder of her coffee, Clara glanced across the street at the sign that read 'Lighthouse Tours.' Beside the store was a dock with boats subtly bobbing as a crew of men hosed the boats down. She inhaled the aroma of her hazelnut coffee and sat daydreaming about starting over in Solomons Island. "Was it a good idea?" she asked herself. Or was she continuing a propitious cycle of working to get a paycheck but neglecting her dreams? What were her dreams, anyway? It was time for Clara to do a lot of soul searching, unfortunately time was not on her side.

Oh, Joan. What should I do? she thought to herself.

Just then Mackenzie returned.

"I saw you staring outside in a daze. You look tired and I know you have to be stressed. Don't torment yourself with this, it's not worth it. I'm packing up a hot lunch for you to take back to the house. It's on me. I want you to take some time for yourself today. Take a hot bath, take a stroll on the beach... I don't care what you do, but take a minute to regroup and decide what you really want for yourself."

Mackenzie walked around to Clara's side of the counter.

"No matter what, I'm here for you. And if you don't call me to help load up the moving truck, I'll never speak to you again."

"You have my word on that one. I need all the help I can get."

"Good."

She gave Clara a hug and then left her to head back to the kitchen.

CHAPTER 5

"Hi there, I'm calling back about the condo for rent in Solomons Landing. I saw it yesterday, and I was wondering if it's still available?"

"It sure is, may I ask who's calling?"

"Clara Covington."

"Yes, Ms. Covington, I remember you. The condo is yours if you're prepared to fill out some paperwork and leave a deposit."

"I'm prepared to stop by today, but I forgot to ask about your pet policy. Are pets allowed?" Clara asked.

"Yes, small dogs and cats are allowed, but the owner is asking for an additional two-hundred-and-fifty-dollar deposit. What kind of pet do you have?"

"A Boston Terrier. She's only twenty pounds and she's super friendly," Clara reassured the property manager.

"Ok, well, just let me know when you're ready to stop by. We can set up everything today and have your keys ready for you this afternoon if you'd like."

Clara felt a sense of relief at the sound of being able to pick up her keys this afternoon. Sure, the place was more expensive than she originally hoped, but it was safe and also relatively close to work. Clara drew a line in the sand with her toes and then turned around to look back toward Joan's house. It was official. Tonight, she would finish packing up and say her final goodbyes to the Russell residence.

"This afternoon sounds perfect. I can be there within the hour," Clara said.

Back at the house, Clara tiptoed gingerly past the living room as not to disturb Olivia and her brother who were laughing and talking over paperwork. Her brother was a handsome guy with dark hair and a gorgeous wife who looked like a model. Clara caught a glimpse of them upon their arrival yesterday. The kids could be heard running nonstop throughout the house and stomping above her head.

"Hey, lady, what are you doing?" a little boy asked.

Clara turned around to see a cute face with freckles staring at her as if she were an intruder.

"Jonathan, come here, please," Olivia called out.

"Yes, Aunt Olivia."

"Sit with your dad for a moment while I talk to our housekeeper, Ms. Clara."

"Ok," he said.

Did she just say our housekeeper? Clara thought to herself.

"Clara, I'd like a moment with you," Olivia said.

"Sure."

"Since we're only two days away, I thought I'd check in with you regarding the plans for Friday. I placed an order for the catering, so all of that is set. However, I'll need you to make a run to the store to ensure we have a few other things."

"Olivia, about that."

"I know it seems like a lot to pull together in a couple of days, but I know you can handle it. It's the unfortunate thing about funerals. No one can ever really plan for things like this," she rambled.

"Olivia, I'm not going to be here to receive the guests. I've decided that attending Joan's funeral is much more important."

"I thought we went over this already. There's no way that we can be ready to receive everyone in time if someone isn't here to make sure everything is in order. I know you were fond of Joan, but I'm sure if she were still here, she would understand."

"Respectfully, that's no longer my concern."

"And you call yourself a friend of Joan's?" Olivia attempted to throw shade over Clara's character, but Clara stood her ground.

"Yes, which is exactly why I plan to be there to pay my respects. Something you don't seem to know much about. I shouldn't have to debate with you about this. Joan meant the world to me. She became, not just my employer, but like family to me when I moved to Maryland. Now, I can stop by the store and have everything you need here at the house, but I'm going on Friday and that's my final word."

"It's going to cost you the bonus, Clara. I'm sorry, but I'm not paying you for work that you won't do."

"The bonus has nothing to do with this. You were offering me the bonus to compensate for asking me to get out with such short notice," Clara lowered voice so her nephew and brother wouldn't hear.

"Well, I've changed my mind. You've had a poor attitude from the moment I arrived. I think it's best we wrap this up as quickly as possible in order to avoid any further conflict. Besides, I know your type. I can smell your motive a mile away. You were probably planning to mooch off the family and stay here as long as you could. If I know right, you were probably doing the same with Aunt Joan. Whoever heard of a housekeeper living in a two thousand square foot basement apartment, rent free, and still receiving a full-time salary? Poor Aunt Joan. She was probably too blind to recognize she was being taken advantage of."

Clara gasped for air. She tried to respond, but the words wouldn't come out. Never in her life had she been accused of taking advantage of anyone. She looked down at the little boy who returned with a toy soldier in hand.

"Aunt Olivia, are you going to come back and play with me?"

"I'll be there in a minute, buddy. Run and be with daddy, I'll be right there."

Once the boy was clear out of sight, Clara turned to Olivia.

"Screw your bonus check. Instead, I'll give you a bonus and have my things out of the house by tomorrow evening at the latest. Good day to you."

Clara walked calmly to the staircase leading to the basement with intentions of disappearing for the remainder of the day.

~

Back at the café, Mike slid into a chair at Mackenzie's station. The place was buzzing more than usual with the aroma of lobster bisque in the air, which was the lunch special for the day. Mackenzie served one customer and rang up another customer's bill before making her way over to Mike.

"Good to see you, Mike. What can I get for you today? Your usual?"

"Mack, you know me all too well, except I think I'm going to add the fried fish sandwich and take my order to go," he said.

"Busy day? You never take your food to go."

"Busy is an understatement. One of my guys has been out

sick for days now, which leaves me shorthanded. I really need to hire someone to help out with the tours. I just hadn't gotten around to it yet. Speaking of hiring someone, I have a question to ask after you're done putting in my order."

"Ask away. Josh will take the order to the back for me, won't you, Josh?" Mackenzie implied.

"Sure, it's not like I'm busy or anything," he teased.

Mackenzie patted him on the back.

"I can always count on Josh to have my back. I owe you one, buddy. Thanks."

"Mmm hmm. Mike you better keep your eye on this one. She's a piece of work," Josh said as he walked away.

The corner of Mike's mouth raised slightly while he shook his head.

"I don't know why you two are always giving each other such a hard time. You know what they say about two people who go at it like that?" He laughed.

"You better not be implying what I think you're trying to imply. Just remember, I'm the one who makes your milkshakes," Mackenzie teased.

"Yes, you do. Therefore, I'll leave that alone. I will, however, ask you about Clara Covington."

Mackenzie's eyes lit up.

"Yes! I heard you offered her a job."

"So, you had a chance to talk to her?" Mike sounded surprised.

"You know we're good friends, right?"

"She did mention the two of you knew each other. It's one of the reasons I felt comfortable enough to offer her the position. I probably should've run it by you before offering her the job. I've just been so swamped that I'm kind of desperate at this point."

"Mike, do not worry about a thing. Clara is super reliable and everybody I know loves her. I mean, what's not to love? She's smart, kind, and she has an amazing track record of working for the last ten years with the same employer. Plus, she's loyal. We wouldn't even be having this conversation if Joan were still here."

"Yeah, she told me about the situation with her boss. It's such a shame."

"It is. She'll be ok. Clara is strong and resilient. She'll make the best of the situation and turn lemons into lemonade. She always does."

"That's good to hear. I knew I had a good vibe about her when we met but having your rubber stamp of approval makes me feel even better." Mike smiled.

"Well, you should because you hired the best. I think you'll work well together. I was just telling her you guys are like two peas in a pod."

"How's that?" Mike asked.

"You both come here at least once a week, if not more, and you order the same thing every single time. If either of you deviates from your usual order, there's usually something stressful going on in your life. It's like you're an open book. I can always tell when something is not right," Mackenzie said.

"Everyone has their quirks, I guess," Mike responded.

"Yeah, but not usually the same quirks."

"There's more?" he asked.

"Oh, I haven't even cracked the surface. But since you two are going to be working together, I'm sure you'll discover some of those quirks for yourself."

Mackenzie laughed out loud.

"It's a shame I hadn't thought of introducing you to Clara before now. It didn't really dawn on me until she told me about the job."

"Hmm, interesting." Mike seemed curious to know more but didn't press the subject.

~

"Ms. Covington, I just have one more paper for you to sign and then I'll get the keys for you. If you have any further questions, I'm usually here every day from nine to five," the clerk said as she passed a clipboard to Clara.

"Actually, before I start making phone calls, I was wondering if you could recommend a company to rent a moving truck from?" she asked.

"I have plenty of recommendations to choose from. The guys always leave a ton of business cards behind. Here, call this company. They've always been able to help my clients whenever they needed someone in a pinch."

"Thank you."

"Sure, no problem. I think you're all set. Here's your keys and the remote control for the front gate. If you'd like, you can leave your car here and take a stroll across the grounds to check out where everything is located. Your apartment is move-in ready if you'd like to go and take a look."

"Thank you so much for everything. I think I will take a peek, just so I can envision how I want to set up everything."

"Perfect. All the best to you, and again, if you need anything, please don't hesitate to let me know."

"Will do."

Clara walked across the quad to the area where her apartment was located. It was a beautiful spring day with a gentle breeze that flowed from the Patuxent, just a few miles beyond a nearby forest. The one perk about her new apartment was the small balcony that would allow her to see the river from a distance. Clara was going to miss the beach, but the balcony would be a wonderful place to start a new ritual of morning meditation.

When she arrived at the third-floor apartment, she turned the key and was greeted by the bright sunshine. The aroma of fresh paint nearly took her breath away, but she knew with the help of some fresh air and maybe a few candles, the odor wouldn't last long. She passed the kitchen to her left and a bedroom on the opposite end of the hall to head straight for the balcony. The apartment was a total of eight hundred square feet, exactly half the size of Joan's basement. It was the only place within her budget that had additional storage space, so she was determined to make it work. She stopped to inhale the fresh air and take in the views. Next, she would need to secure a truck to rent in the morning and call Mike to confirm her start date.

On the drive to the truck rental place, Clara activated her Bluetooth and dialed the number to Lighthouse Tours.

"Lighthouse Tours, how may I help you?" Mike answered.

"Hi, Mike. It's Clara, your new assistant."

"Clara, what a pleasant surprise. I was just talking to Mackenzie about you."

"Really? In that case, I'm sure you know my whole life story by now." Clara laughed.

"Ha, not quite. She had nothing but great things to say about you."

"That's good to know."

"I wasn't expecting to hear from you so early. Is everything okay?" he asked.

"Yes, actually everything is moving along better than expected. I'm making plans to move in the morning, and I figured this might be a good time to call and confirm a start date."

"So soon? I thought you wanted to give yourself at least a week to get unpacked and settled in," Mike said.

"Originally, I was thinking the same. But to be honest, the longer I wait to start means the longer I wait to get paid. I can always unpack over the weekend."

"Well, if that's the case you won't get any arguments out of me. I need all the help I can get. How does eight o'clock on Monday morning sound?"

"It sounds like music to my ears. Thank you for the opportunity, Mike. I appreciate it."

"Don't thank me too fast. You might have regrets on Monday when you see how busy we are."

"The best way to learn is to dive right in, right? Don't worry, I'm pretty tough. I can handle it."

"Good, then I look forward to seeing you on Monday."

"All right, see you then."

She pressed the button on her steering wheel to disconnect the call. Clara breathed a sigh of relief. Given the way the week began, things were finally beginning to take shape. Now, if she could just figure out how to get her things boxed up and in a truck by the a.m., she knew everything would be all right.

CHAPTER 6

"Mack, can you toss me a roll of packing tape? I have one last box over here in the corner that needs some extra tape, and then we can get out of here."

"Think fast," Mackenzie said as she pitched the tape across the room.

"Thanks. Hey, maybe we can grab a sandwich on the way to the apartment. It will be noon by the time we pull out of here. I'm sure you'll be hungry by then."

"That's not a bad idea. I normally take my lunch break by twelve, anyway."

"I appreciate you taking time off to help me today. I couldn't have done this without you," Clara said.

"I know you would do the same for me."

Just then the women were interrupted by the sound of footsteps descending into the basement. Olivia appeared and surveyed the stacks of boxes around the room.

Olivia had the appearance of a businesswoman who worked on Wall Street. She always dressed in a pantsuit with high end shoes and accessories with nowhere to go. Clara briefly recalled the stories Joan told about this imaginary life that Olivia lived in her head, where everybody believed she was rich and famous. Rumor had it she was a former mortgage broker, one of the best in her field. She gave it all up when she fell in love with one of the top brokers in her division. He offered her the lifestyle she always wanted. A fancy car and a big house, minus children, because that would be too much work. "If she was really rich, she wouldn't have to flaunt it so much," she recalled Joan saying.

Famous for what? Pampering herself and being the most self-centered individual on the face of this earth? Clara thought.

Mackenzie waited for Clara to speak up, but it was clear she was in a daze.

"Can I help you?" Mackenzie asked.

"You can start by telling me your name. I haven't seen you around here before," Olivia snarled.

Clara spoke up.

"This is my friend, Mackenzie. She's here to help me move my things. Is there something you need, Olivia?"

Olivia gave Mackenzie the once over before proceeding.

"Yes, I'd like to speak to you upstairs, if you have a minute."

"There isn't anything that can't be said in front of Mackenzie. I'm all ears. What's up?"

"All right, then. I have a few legal documents I'd like you to sign."

"Ma'am?" Clara couldn't imagine what she could be referring to.

"It's important that we terminate your position the proper way. You know, just to be certain we don't have any legal matters that surface down the line," Olivia said.

"What kind of legal matters?"

"It's just a simple form that states you decided to leave early, denied your bonus pay, and you won't try to return to the

property or pursue any legal action against the family estate."
Olivia placed a pen and the papers on the box in front of her.

"Eh em." Mackenzie cleared her throat while giving Clara
a look.

"Olivia, I have to say, you never cease to amaze me. I
thought maybe there would be a chance that we could end on a
peaceful note."

"I'm coming to you in peace, but who's to say down the line
you won't decide to turn on the family? I would think for the
sake of Joan's memory, you wouldn't do such a thing, but one
can ever be too sure."

While Clara looked at Olivia in utter disbelief, Mackenzie
stepped forward and spoke up for her.

"Olivia, I know this is none of my business," she began.

"Then stay out of it." Olivia snapped.

"As her friend, I'm not going to do that. Clara is exhausted.
The last forty-eight hours have been filled with very little sleep
and a lot of stress and worry. Perhaps she can take your papers,
have them reviewed by her lawyer, and get back to you."

All three women stood quietly, waiting for the other to
respond. Finally, Clara asked Olivia to leave the papers for her
to review.

"I'm sure you can give me a few days to get settled. I'll
make it a priority to look things over next week and get back to
you," Clara said in a monotone voice.

"Fine. Be sure to leave your copy of the keys in the foyer
before you go." Olivia stormed off in her Louis Vuitton heels,
never to be seen for the remainder of the day.

~

Clara mashed the brakes of the smelly U-Haul truck while
backing into a space. Her brunette friend pulled in the next

parking spot, driving old Bessy, with her cool sunglasses on. Clara considered how thankful she was for her friend's support and positive outlook. Mackenzie always saw the good in life and in others. The glass was always half full in her opinion and according to her, this situation would be no different.

"I don't know about you, but I say we take a break to eat these sandwiches and then get started. Maybe we'll get lucky and catch a couple of guys who wouldn't mind lending a helping hand," Mackenzie said.

"Sounds good. If you grab the sandwich bags, I'll grab the soda cases, and we can spread out on the living room floor and have ourselves a picnic."

"You have fun with that. I'm going to check out the balcony breeze you've been raving about," Mackenzie said while heading upstairs.

"What was I thinking? The balcony is a perfect place for lunch. Just don't let me get too comfortable. We still have a lot to do, and I can easily see myself taking an afternoon nap."

"You and me both, girl," Mackenzie agreed.

The girls spread out on the balcony to eat and continue their conversation.

"So, how does it feel to have your own place now?" Mackenzie asked.

"I don't know, to be honest with you. For starters, it's empty, and I know that will change, but it feels like a strange place to me. It just makes me think of Joan and how much life has changed in such a quick period of time," Clara responded.

"She became more like a mother figure to you, didn't she?"

"A mother figure, a friend. You name it. Right before I moved to Maryland, losing my parents was the worst thing that could've ever happened to me. I'll never forget the sound in the officer's voice when he shared the news of their accident. To this day if I could get a hold of the drunk driver who took them away from me, I don't know what I'd do to him."

Clara wiped her eyes.

"My self-centered sister wasn't making things any better. You would think she would've been there to help with all the arrangements. But no, not Agnes. She barely spoke two words. That was a time when we needed each other most," Clara said.

"I guess everybody deals with grief differently."

"Yeah, I guess. She managed to speak up when she thought there would be something to collect from their insurance policies. What a fool! They had enough to cover the cost of their funeral and that was it. Our parents weren't wealthy. They were hard working and provided us with the most valuable gift of all, their love. Clearly, that wasn't enough for her. I'll bet momma would be so disappointed to see the person she has become. And Olivia is no different. She and my sister are like twins from another mother."

"Ahh, I get it," Mack said while setting her soda down.

"What do you get?" Clara asked.

"That explains why you have so much venom toward Olivia. She reminds you of your sister."

"I'd like to think that I know how to separate the two. My relationship with Olivia isn't nearly as personal. They just remind me of one another, that's all. Joan and I used to swap stories for hours. Now, I see first-hand what she was talking about. When I responded to Joan's ad for a housekeeper, I was looking for an escape. I'll be forever grateful for the way she took me in. I didn't even have housekeeping experience when she hired me." Clara laughed.

"Hmm, well isn't that funny. Here you are ten years later starting over with a new job opportunity, in a new field with no experience. You always manage to find triumph out of tragedy." Mackenzie leaned closer.

"You're blessed, Clara. Never forget that," she said.

"I can't disagree with you. I was on the verge of calling my sister, and now I'm sitting here on my new balcony with a job waiting for me on Monday morning." Clara smiled.

"Speaking of your new job, I saw Mike this week. He seems really excited to have you on board at Lighthouse Tours."

"Thanks for putting in a good word for me," Clara said.

"Oh, I told him how much of a hot mess you can be, but I guess he decided to hire you anyway," she teased.

"Mack! Come on, I know better. You didn't say that to him."

"Of course, I didn't. I told him he won't regret the decision. You should've seen the way his eyes lit up when I told him how much the two of you were alike."

Clara swatted at Mackenzie's arm and threatened to pour a small drop of soda on her head.

"Don't you dare, Clara. I promise, you'll regret it," Mackenzie said.

"I won't pour it if you promise to stop trying to play match-maker once and for all. Mike and I will never be an item, the same way Josh and I will never be an item. You got it?" she said with a smirk.

"Okay, okay. You don't have to be so hostile." Mackenzie surrendered.

"Now, let's see if we can get this truck unpacked before five o'clock. I have to pick up my baby girl from daycare by five at the latest."

As they were helping each other up off the floor of the balcony, Clara turned toward Mackenzie.

"Mack, thanks for being such a good friend," she said.

"You don't have to thank me. Just take it easy when we're lugging that mattress up the flight of stairs."

"Ha! I will."

~

Later, that evening Clara made a final trip to the house to give it the once over, pick up Holly, and drop off the keys. She didn't run into Olivia anymore, nor did she care to.

Back at the apartment, the boxes and bags were stacked a mile high. She had to establish a pathway just to get from one end of the place to the other. She sat on the floor in pure exhaustion with a box of pizza and Holly by her side.

"Poor Holly. This place is ten times smaller than what you're used to, isn't it, girl?"

Holly wagged her tail and settled down next to Clara.

"Now, if I could just figure out where I put my clothes for the funeral tomorrow," Clara said to herself.

Thankfully her bed was set up and her furniture was in place, but she was a long way off from creating an oasis that she could call home.

While searching around for her clothing box, Clara mashed the buttons to dial her voicemail.

"You have five missed messages," the automated voice said.

"Hello, Clara. This is Mrs. Walker. We met earlier this week about the housekeeping position. I had a chance to review your references, and I'd like to offer you the position. Please call me back as soon as possible. I have other candidates waiting to hear back if you're not interested."

Clara immediately hit the delete button.

"Sorry, lady, no can do. You weren't exactly warm and welcoming," she said aloud.

The next message was from an unfamiliar man with a stern voice.

"Mrs. Covington. This is Dale from Davidson and Associates. Please call me back at your earliest convenience.

Your presence is requested for a very important matter regarding the Russell estate." He abruptly hung up.

This time she hit the save button.

That little witch. Was it really going to kill Olivia to wait a week before she started calling her lawyer! Clara thought to herself.

The last couple of messages were more opportunities to interview for housekeeping positions, but Clara breezed right past them. If nothing else had come out of this, it was becoming more obvious by the minute that it was time for a major change.

Clara watched as Holly curled up and nodded off to sleep near the couch. She then surveyed the room looking for the boxes labeled clothing. She may not find the outfit she was planning to wear, but as long as she looked presentable, it would have to do.

After plunging into several clothing boxes, Clara came across a navy floral printed dress with a narrow belt to hug her waistline. It was a birthday gift from Joan. She always tried to encourage Clara to spruce herself up and go out and meet someone. Sadly, Clara never had the opportunity to wear it until now, which was all the more reason to wear it in Joan's honor. It would be her tribute to the wonderful woman who gave her a fresh start.

Clara fluffed the dress and placed in on a hanger to let it air out.

"Joan, you always did have good taste. I'll wear it tomorrow in honor of you," she said aloud while standing back and admiring the dress.

Her next priority would be to nibble on the rest of her pizza and bathe, but not before stretching across her mattress and staring at the popcorn ceiling.

"Cheers to new beginnings," she whispered before closing her eyes and drifting off to sleep.

CHAPTER 7

"*L*adies and gentlemen, if Aunt Joan were here, I know she wouldn't stand for a somber gathering of mourners. She would encourage us to celebrate her life and celebrate the lives of those who are still here with us. I could always count on Aunt Joan to be there when I needed her. We were so close, and I'm going to miss her terribly. Today, I beg you to be there for each other. Hold your loved ones near and dear to your heart and tell them you love them." Olivia bowed her head toward the end of her emotional speech.

Clara subtly glanced around to see if anyone was buying what Olivia was saying. She agreed with a good portion of it, but the part about them being close was a far cry from what Joan used to say.

Clara rose from the pew to sing the closing hymn. Memories of her parents came rushing over her as she tried to follow along. There was something about these occasions that always caused her to reflect on how she chose to live her life. Could she do a better job of trying to maintain a bond with her sister?

Clara reflected upon her family relationships, knowing that her parents would've wanted better.

At the conclusion of the service, several people remained in the lobby paying their respect to the family. Clara tried to slip out unnoticed but was stopped by Olivia just outside the chapel.

"Clara, may I have a word with you?" Olivia asked.

Clara's car was just a few feet away. She wanted nothing more than to keep on walking and pretend she didn't hear her.

"Yes, Olivia."

"Thank you for coming today," she said.

"Certainly, I wouldn't miss it. You know that."

"Yes, I stopped you because I was wondering if you heard from the lawyer regarding the family estate?"

"Olivia, for the last time, if you just give me a few days to get settled, I promise to review your paperwork and get back to you," Clara said, sounding annoyed.

"I'd appreciate the paperwork as soon as possible, but that's not was I was referring to. It's been brought to my attention that your presence is requested at the reading of Aunt Joan's will. Surely you received a call about it by now?"

Clara stuttered. "I... I received a message from a lawyer, but I haven't had time to call him back," she said.

"Oh, well. I wouldn't invest too much time and energy into anything the lawyer has to say. My brother and I will fight tooth and nail over what's rightfully ours. Nothing personal, but the only people who truly belong at the reading is the family, and that's it," Olivia warned.

"What are you talking about, Olivia? No one has ever said a word to me about Joan's will. This is the first I'm hearing anything about it."

"Well, I'll spare you the details and let you talk to him for yourself. Just know that we're not backing down. We will defend and protect what's ours. It's just too bad Aunt Joan couldn't discern the kind of person you really are before she passed away." Olivia stormed off and disappeared into the crowd.

Clara was dumbfounded by her remarks. *What had she done to make anyone question her character?* she thought to herself.

She turned and walked toward the car in utter disbelief. It was clear she would have to put in a phone call to the lawyer to understand what was really going on. But, why is Olivia acting so hostile? she wondered.

~

On Monday, Clara woke to the ringing of her alarm. It was her first day of work at the new job and she had every intention of being early. She still hadn't heard back from the lawyer's office after calling over the weekend, but there was no time to dwell on that now. The only thing she had in mind was walking Holly, grabbing a quick granola bar, and heading out the door.

Around seven-thirty, she pulled into a parking space in front of Lighthouse Tours. The lights were on and Mike was already busy walking around near the front window. Out of nervous energy she slammed the car door and marched ahead with her curls bouncing behind her. From across the street, she could hear a loud whistle that caused her to turn around.

"Knock 'em dead, tiger," Mackenzie yelled.

That was all Clara needed to relax and crack a smile. She truly was a natural born model from head to toe. She wore the same dress from Friday, with a touch of rouge lipstick and let her curls flow down past her bosom.

"Thanks, Mack. Have a great day," she yelled back.

Once inside, she greeted Mike in a melodious voice. "Good morning."

"Hey, Clara. Wow!" Mike's stunned appearance threw Clara off guard.

"Eh em. I meant to say, good morning. You surprised me. You are a half hour early." He sounded like he was overcorrecting himself, but she went along with it.

"I figured if I arrived early, I could observe your morning routines," she said.

"Routines, right. Uh, come on in and make yourself comfortable. We have a locker area in the back for personal belongings. I set aside one with your name labeled on the front. Of course, we always begin the day with a cup of coffee. It's the only way to start the day around here. I was just about to grab a cup. Would you like some?"

"Yes, I would love a cup. Thank you," she responded.

"Awesome, how do you like your coffee?" Mike stood smiling nervously like he'd never seen a beautiful girl before.

"I take my coffee black."

"So do I. See, I knew this would work. I like you already," he said.

Mike placed the carafe in the coffee machine and hit a button to begin brewing a fresh pot.

"I don't mind getting the coffee started for us when I arrive in the morning. All you have to do is say the word," Clara said while placing her purse in the locker.

"I appreciate it. Jonathan usually looks for a cup when he arrives around ten. You'll meet him later on today. He's one of our tour guides."

"Okay, sounds great," she said.

"Before I let it slip my mind, did you have a chance to stop by the auto body shop this weekend? I still feel terrible about your headlamp."

"Yes, about that. Al says it no big deal. He's going to fix it Wednesday morning, and it will be like nothing ever happened."

Clara breathed a sigh of relief.

"Excellent, did he say how much it would cost?"

"Yes, but it's nothing worth mentioning. His prices are dirt cheap. I'd rather you focus on getting your repairs done. Your car took much more of a beating than mine did," he offered.

"Absolutely not. I take full responsibility for what I did. You could deduct it from my first paycheck if you'd like," she argued.

Mike passed her a hot cup of coffee.

"Here. We have a busy day ahead of us. Why don't we talk about this later?" he said as he led Clara back to the front desk.

She followed behind him trying not to notice his broad shoulders.

He's your boss, Clara. Stay focused. This is exactly what you get for not dating for so long. First time you get around a good-looking man, you can't even think straight. Focus, she thought to herself.

"Okay, I'm going to start by showing you the most important book of all. It's the appointment book. If you can master our scheduling process, then you'll be well on your way to mastering everything else around here."

"Okay." She carefully examined this week's appointments.

"Lighthouse Tours attracts tourists who will pay by the hour to tour around the area by boat. Our tours run all the way north as far as Annapolis. We have fishing tours, dinner tours, lighthouse tours, you name it. All you have to do is ensure that you stick to the available time slots and available capacity, which is written right here for you. For example, the five o'clock tour next Friday can host no more than ten people. Make sense?" he asked.

"It makes a lot of sense. I think I can handle this."

"Good. Now the only other thing you have to do is qualify the tourist by asking this set of questions over here. Here's how you respond if they answer yes, and here's what you say if they answer no," Mike explained.

Clara looked at Mike with confidence. She had a yellow legal pad in hand just in case she needed to jot down notes.

"Scheduling doesn't sound bad at all. If any questions pop up, I'll jot them down and check with you later. What would you like for me to do in between scheduling?"

"I'm glad you asked. I have a stack of time sheets for the guys that I've been meaning to enter into the system. We're actually changing over to a more computerized way of keeping records but until everything is set up, I just need you to record their total hours for the week and hit save, right here. Trust me. It's so easy my grandmother could do it." He chuckled.

Their conversation was interrupted by Jonathan, one of the workers in charge of running the fishing tours. He was the expert at all things related to fish. He always seemed to know the right time to put out his line and catch a net load of fish. As a result, Mike put him in charge of the fishing tours to ensure his clients would have an experience to remember.

"Howdy, there folks," Jonathan said as he removed his hat.

"Hey, Jonathan. What are you doing here so early? I thought your shift doesn't start until ten?" Mike asked.

"Not so, boss. My first tour heads out at nine a.m. I figured I'd give the boat and the equipment the once over before heading out." He turned to Clara and gave her a nod.

"Where's my manners? Jonathan, this is Clara, she's our new assistant," Mike said.

Clara extended her hand from behind the desk to greet Jonathan.

62

"Hi there, Jonathan. You look very familiar. Have we met before?" she asked.

"We could have. My last name is Mulligan. I believe I've seen your friendly face around. Perhaps at the café?"

"Yes, that's it. You always ask for Mackenzie's booth when you come in." She smiled.

"I wouldn't have it any other way." He chuckled.

"That makes two of us. Mackenzie is my best friend."

Jonathan tapped Mike on the arm. "Why didn't you mention that, Mike? Anybody who's good enough for Mackenzie is good with me. Welcome aboard. Say, don't let this fella drive you crazy on your first day. There will be plenty of time to learn all the ins and outs of this place," Jonathan said.

He then turned and looked at Mike. After nodding his head and chuckling to himself, he proceeded to head to the back of the store.

"I'll be out back if you need me," he yelled back and then disappeared, leaving Mike and Clara alone.

"Jonathan is a great guy. You're going to love the staff here. My guess is you've already met most of them and you don't even know it yet."

"Perhaps. I'm embarrassed to admit that I've spent the last several years being a homebody except for taking occasional outings to the café. That's how Mack and I got to become such good friends," she said.

"That's right, prior to this job you worked as a housekeeper, didn't you?"

"Yes. A live-in housekeeper," Clara responded.

"It must be hard to divide your time when you live and work in the same place. Pretty all-consuming, no?"

"I guess." Clara didn't quite agree but didn't want to invest too much energy on the topic. It was a choice she made over the years to hide from the world and consume herself with work. Joan always tried to encourage her to do differently.

"Well, there will be plenty of time for us to get to chat further. I'm going to head to the back and scour my desk for everyone's work schedule. If Jonathan has a tour at nine, I suspect I may have screwed up Brody's schedule as well."

"Brody?" she repeated.

"Yes, Brody takes care of maintenance, and Ms. Mae handles the dinner tours. She's itching to get back out there after being out with knee surgery. She kinda reminds me of a wise yet cool grandma, very youthful and spunky. But, if you call her grandma to her face, she'll never let you hear the end of it. So, take my advice and don't do it."

"Note to self. Do not call Ms. Mae grandma. Got it." Clara winked.

"All right, are you good? Do you have any questions for me?" he asked.

"No, but I promise not to hold back if I think of anything."

Clara made herself comfortable in her roll-around chair while watching Mike back out of the room.

"Okay, just holler if you need me," he said, almost tripping right over a stack of boxes inconveniently positioned near the doorway.

Clara tried to keep a straight face and refrain from giggling at his clumsy behavior. She wouldn't dare repeat this to Mack for fear that she'd make something of it, but there was a tiny electric spark between the two of them. One that would have to be ignored, of course, but nevertheless, it was there.

❧

Out back, near the dock, Mike caught up with Jonathan to have him sign off on his time sheet. He found him moseying around in his waders while looking through his equipment. Jonathan believed that getting in the water and getting dirty was the best part of the tour. There had to be something to it because he always had tons of takers lined up to go on his fishing tours.

"Jonathan, if you'd be so kind as to put your John Hancock right here, sir, then I can see to it that you get paid," Mike said while passing him a clipboard.

"Yes, sir." He chuckled.

"What's so funny? You've been grinning ever since I introduced you to Clara," Mike asked.

"Me?" Jonathan teased.

"Yeah, you. There's no one else standing out here right now but you. Now let me have it. What's on your mind?"

"Well, for starters, is that the girl you got into the fender bender with?" Jonathan asked.

"Yeah, that's her. Why?"

Jonathan laughed even harder than before.

"You're in knee deep, my friend. Knee deep!"

Mike looked up to Jonathan. He always imparted words of wisdom when he spoke, and he was older than Mike, which meant his wisdom came from experience.

"I was buried knee deep in work before she arrived. I'm hoping that having her join the team will help alleviate that," Mike said.

"That's not what I'm talking about Mike and you know it. You've got a crush on that girl. I could tell by the way you described her when you told us about the accident. Your face nearly lit the sky when you spoke about her. Then, there's this morning. When I walked through the door you were grinning like a Cheshire cat. You've got it bad." Jonathan slapped Mike on the shoulder and returned to his equipment.

Mike was speechless at first.

"Come on, Jonathan. I have to be nice to her, it's her first day. That doesn't mean I like her. What kind of boss would I be if I was mean to my employees?" Mike asked.

"Ms. Mae doesn't hardly get the same kind of attention. You forget that I've been around the block a time or two. I'm not as young as I used to be, but I know that look. Hell, I probably invented the look." He chuckled.

"I don't know what look you're talking about. I'm just doing my job and keeping things strictly professional. You're the one that probably has the hots for her. It's been a long time since we had a beautiful young lady in the office," Mike said.

"Strike one. You just admitted she's beautiful," Jonathan teased.

"That's it. I'm out of here. Thanks for your signature." Mike turned around to head back inside.

Jonathan practiced throwing his line in the water and continued laughing loud enough for Mike to hear him.

"Have a good tour, Jonathan," Mike hollered while walking away. *Yeah, sure,* he thought, *Clara is pretty.* A guy would have to be blind to miss her hourglass figure, voluptuous bust, and her smile that lit up a room. He noticed it the day he met her, but never thought she'd actually follow through and apply for the job. He'd have to find a way to keep his thoughts at bay. Now that she was on board at Lighthouse Tours, being an ultimate professional was his top priority.

~

For her lunch break, Clara strolled toward the nearest public bench which gave her the perfect view of the boats that were docked nearby. She considered stopping by the café, but Clara needed to be realistic about her budget now more than ever. Instead, she packed her favorite Boars Head turkey sandwich, a Coke, and a handful of grapes to hold her over till the end of the day. She had exactly fifty minutes to spare, so she decided to try and reach out to Dale, the lawyer, one last time.

"Davidson and Associates," a woman answered.

"Hi, my name is Clara Covington. I've been trying to get in touch with Dale, but unfortunately, we've been playing phone tag."

"Yes, Ms. Covington. Dale has been trying to reach you. He just went up to his office. If you'll hold on a moment, I'll connect the call," she said.

"Thank you."

A couple of minutes passed before Dale greeted Clara.

"Ms. Covington, how are you?"

"I'm well, thank you. My apologies for not being able to connect with you sooner. I had to move this weekend and well, no excuses, but life has been a little hectic over the last couple of weeks," Clara said.

"No explanation needed. I completely understand. My wife and I recently moved as well. We're empty nesters and thought now that the kids are gone, it might be a good time to downsize. It sounded like a good idea in theory, but after discovering how much stuff we accumulated over the years, I was ready to throw in the towel and give up on moving altogether."

"Oh, boy, that sounds like quite the undertaking."

"It was," Dale replied.

"But, enough about me. I've been trying to get in touch with you regarding Joan's estate."

Clara interrupted. "I know, I know, Olivia has been after me to sign some legal documents stating that I will never try to sue the family or make any claims against them, and yada yada. I really don't understand why she feels the need to take things this far."

"Interesting. Well, that's not what I was going to say, but

thank you for making me aware. I can't offer any legal advice, but I would caution you about signing anything until you have the opportunity to attend the reading of Joan's will. Your name has been included in the estate, and I would think you'd like to learn more about that first before making any decisions."

Clara was confused.

"Eh, Joan included me in her will?" she asked.

"She did. Although I have to follow precise instructions about withholding the details until everyone gathers on Friday, but, she did include you. We were originally supposed to meet today, but the meeting was rescheduled for Friday at nine o'clock. It will be right here at my office at Davidson & Associates. Will you be able to make it?"

Clara fumbled over her words. All sorts of thoughts were running through her mind about the last time Joan asked her to drive her to the lawyer's office. Of course, she wouldn't have had a clue as to why she went that day. She just remembered it was one of her last outings anywhere before she became really sick.

"Uh, yeah. I guess. I just started a new job, so I'll have to make arrangements with my boss, but I'm sure something can be worked out," Clara responded.

"Excellent. Let me give you the address."

"I know where you are. I've been outside your building before," she said.

"Oh, wonderful. Well, then, that settles everything. I'll see you Friday at nine, sharp. In the meantime, if anything pops up, please let me know," he said.

"I wonder if Joan left instructions for me to take care of her dog, Holly? It's not like Olivia wanted anything to do with her. She was quick to hand her over to me so I could find her a new forever home," Clara stated.

"Again, Ms. Covington, I'm under strict obligation to share

the details of the will on Friday. By law, everyone must be present and proper documents will need to be signed."

"Yes, of course. Dale, one last thing." Clara hesitated.

"Yes?"

"Is Olivia aware of this? Does she know I will be there on Friday? Because if so, I can't imagine that will go over too well with her."

Dale spoke in a much lower voice. He had the raspy tone of a smoker, but you could tell he meant business when he left Clara with these parting words.

"It may not go over well with her, but there isn't a damn thing she can do about it. Period," Dale said.

Clara was speechless. She didn't know much but decided not to press Dale any further. She thanked him for his help and concluded the call.

CHAPTER 8

Clara returned from lunch to find Mike manning the front desk, a woman leaning on the back counter with a coffee mug in hand, and a man, presumably Brody, asking where he could find a stack of maintenance repair logs.

"There she is. You must be the new gal. I'm Mae and this is Brody. Nice to meet you." Ms. Mae extended her hand to Clara and welcomed her with a warm smile. Clara shook hands with Brody, who nodded his head and briefly inspected her appearance.

"It's about time I had someone to help counteract all the testosterone around here." She chuckled. Welcome aboard!" Mae said.

"Thank you!" Clara responded.

Ms. Mae looked to be in her upper fifties. She had dark hair with silver streaks that were starting to emerge at the roots, and she moved with a cane that appeared to be used for moral support more than anything else. Clara assumed it was something she adapted to in connection with her knee surgery.

Brody, on the other hand, looked a little rough around the

edges. Nothing a razor couldn't fix. His hands were dirty like those of a mechanic, but it all made sense given he was in charge of maintaining the boats.

Mike passed Brody the papers he was looking for, and he politely tipped his hat before exiting.

"It was nice meeting you, Ms. Clara. If anyone is looking for me, I'll be out back taking care of the boats. Holler if you need anything," he said.

"Okay, thanks."

Ms. Mae continued asking questions. She seemed head over heels about having a new female employee around and was curious to know more about Clara.

"Rumor has it you're not new to Solomons Island. How is it you've been here for ten years and we haven't crossed paths before? It just doesn't make any sense," Ms. Mae said.

Clara glanced at Mike who was listening intently. It hadn't crossed his mind that he was still sitting in Clara's seat, which is where she needed to be if she was going to get any work done for the afternoon.

"Well, Ms. Mae, I guess I'm to blame for that. Solomons Island is small, but not so small that you couldn't miss a homebody like myself who spent most of her time indoors, taking care of the sick. Maybe occasionally you could catch me strolling on the beach by the Putuxent, but even the area by the house was rather private," Clara said.

"Hmm, okay. A little mysterious, but I'll take it," Ms. Mae teased.

"So, I take it you're more of the quiet type?" She continued.

"Total opposite from you, Ms. Mae," Mike said with a smirk.

Ms. Mae turned around and looked for something to throw at Mike, but the best she could come up with was an eraser.

The two had more of a mother and son kind of relationship, but it was sweet.

"I do have the gift of gab, but you have to if you're going to be a tour guide, don't you think?" Ms. Mae asked Clara.

"I would think the tourists appreciate your friendly personality. I certainly do, Ms. Mae."

"See, Mike. She appreciates my gifts," Ms. Mae mocked.

"Where are you from, dear?" she asked.

"I was born and raised in New York City."

"A city girl? Well, I'll be. I would've never detected it. What on earth brought you out to these rural parts of Maryland? I bet you've seen more pastures, farmland, and water than you've ever seen in your entire life." Ms. Mae got a kick out of her own jokes.

"I love it, to be honest with you. I came here for a change in scenery. It's so peaceful out here. Occasionally, I take nice long drives through the countryside to take in all the natural beauty and count the abandoned barns I find along the way. My favorite pastime is hanging out at the beach, though. Nothing beats the tranquility of being near the water," Clara said.

Clara was still waiting to get to her desk when Mike realized and hopped out of her chair.

"You probably need to get over here, don't you?" he asked.

They both tried to get out of the way but ended up doing a left-to-right dance around one another instead.

Ms. Mae took it all in. Her lip rose with a slow, emerging smile. She recognized that little two step they were doing. She had danced the same dance more than once in her lifetime.

"Mike, would you let the poor girl get to her seat already." She chuckled.

Mike graciously slid over to one side and held out his hand toward the chair.

"Ladies first," he said.

"Thanks, Mike."

"No problem. If it's all right with you, ladies, I'm going to excuse myself and get back to a little bookkeeping. Clara, if you wouldn't mind holding all of my calls for the next hour, that would be great. Tax season is upon us and I want to make sure I'm prepared."

"Hold all of your calls. Got it," she responded.

"Oh, Mike. Before I forget. Something very important came up and I need to ask a favor." She felt foolish asking the boss for a favor on the first week of work, but this was one of those situations that couldn't be avoided.

"Sure, how can I help you?" he asked.

Ms. Mae continued sipping on her coffee as she soaked up every word. Both Clara and Mike glanced her way, hoping she would give them a moment to speak in private.

"Oh, uh, I have something I need to check on in the back. You two talk. Clara, I'll catch up with you later. It was nice meeting you, darlin.'"

"Nice meeting you, too, Ms. Mae." Clara waited for her to clear the room.

Mike fidgeted with a pen, before placing it behind his ear, and folded his arms to listen. Clara felt a little nervous asking him anything, given how much he'd already helped her out. For a moment her mind wandered to how good looking he was. She was curious about what lay underneath his button-down denim shirt. *What is my problem?* she thought to herself. Thankfully, she snapped out of it in time to ask her question.

"I talked to Joan's lawyer today during lunch."

"Joan?" he asked.

"I'm sorry, I may or may not have mentioned her when we met. She's my former boss. The lady who passed away."

"Yes. Is everything okay?" Mike stood upright.

"Everything is fine. Apparently, Joan left me in her will. He wants me to attend the reading of her will on Friday. Honestly, I don't know what to make of it. It surprised me to hear the news. I mean... I already have her dog. Everything else I would imagine goes to the family," Clara babbled.

"You should be honored. You must've been pretty special for her to leave you in her will," he said.

Clara shrugged her shoulders, not knowing what to make of it. The one thing she was certain of was Olivia would not be happy she was there.

"The reading is at nine a.m. It's actually just a mile or so away from here."

"So, you were hoping to come in a little later on Friday morning?" he asked.

"If you wouldn't mind. I promise I won't make a habit of doing things like this."

"Clara, don't apologize, life happens. Take care of business. I'll be here you when you get back... I mean ... we'll be here," Mike corrected himself.

"Thank you. I owe you one."

Just then they were interrupted by the ringing of the office phone.

"Lighthouse Tours," Clara answered.

Mike started mouthing the words "I'll be in the back." Clara gave him the thumbs up and he disappeared to tackle some paperwork.

~

"So, how was your first day?" Mackenzie asked. She listened while feverishly mopping up the sticky tea that had spilled behind the counter.

"It was a little hectic. But, a good kind of hectic, if that makes sense."

"How so?" Mackenzie asked.

"Well, I definitely have my work cut out for me to learn the ropes. There are forms for everything, and sometimes I don't know the answers to the customers' questions, which is to be expected. But, my biggest thing is learning how to multi-task. I'm used to working on one project and then moving on to the next. Once I get the hang of things, I think it will be a lot better."

"Geez. Cut yourself some slack, for God's sake. That just goes to show how much of a perfectionist you are."

"I don't think so. I just hate being the new kid on the block. I'm more of the self-sufficient type. I hate having to ask so many questions. It makes me feel like I'm bothering people, you know?"

"Yeah, well, I'm sure Mike's happy to answer your questions." Mackenzie stopped and lowered her voice.

"It probably makes him feel needed, if you know what I mean."

"I'm not going to even dignify that with an answer. How's your day coming along?"

Clara switched the subject.

"I don't know that it could get any worse. The boss announced this morning he's officially handing the place over to new ownership in a month," Mack grumbled.

"You know how that can go. We're either going to love the new person or start putting out feelers for alternative employment." She continued.

"Yeah, but Mack, this is a good thing, right? New ownership is better than selling the place all together and being out of a job," Clara protested.

Josh walked over with a carafe filled with hot coffee and a slice of cheesecake for Clara.

"Tell the fool something, Clara. I've been trying to

convince her of the same thing all morning, but she won't hear of it from me. Maybe she'll listen to you," he said.

"Thanks for the cake and coffee, Josh. You guys sure do spoil me around here. Yet another reason why I'll accept the new owners over selling. Plus, we get to continue working across the street from each other, Mack. It doesn't get any better than this."

"Hmm, I agree wholeheartedly about that part. However, the two of you better hope and pray this works out. I've worked for plenty of bosses in my day. Some of them were great. My favorites were always the ones who were laid back and let you get your job done without constantly watching over your shoulder." Mack continued to whine.

"True, but come on. You got this. Where's that optimism you're always toting around?" Clara smiled.

"She's right, Mack. Glass is half full, remember?" Josh winked and walked away.

For the first time, it felt like Josh had come to terms with his lingering crush on Clara and finally laid it to rest. Today, their exchange felt more like a regular friendship, and she liked it.

"Hey, Mack," she whispered.

Mackenzie laid down her mop and gave Clara her full attention.

"You will not believe this. Hell, I almost don't believe it. But, I talked to Joan's lawyer today. Turns out she left me in her will," Clara said.

"Really?" Mack soaked up everything that Clara divulged as if she were reading the latest gossip column.

"Yes, and everybody is gathering at his office this Friday for the reading of her will. Everybody, including Olivia," Clara emphasized.

"Good grief. This ought to be a showdown for real. I wish I

could be a fly on the wall for this one. What do you think she left you?" Mackenzie asked.

"The dog, Holly? I don't know. I can't imagine anything major. Even if she did, I'm not about to get into a battle with her wicked niece over it. Absolutely not! I can see her now, threatening me and trying to make my life a living hell. No, ma'am." Clara shook her head.

"I don't give a rat's you know what about her threats. If Joan left you something, then by law, you're entitled to it. Period."

"Now you're sounding like the lawyer. He was quick to remind me of the same thing," Clara said.

"Well, then, there you have it. Case closed. I hope you walk away with way more than a dog. You worked for her for ten years and helped care for her when she was sick."

"And, Joan paid me to do my job. Mack, you know I don't care about fancy things. The only thing of value to me was Joan. All of Joan's possessions could go up in smoke tomorrow, and somehow I think we'd all survive just fine."

"Ha, tell that to Olivia." Mack cocked her head back in laughter. She felt confident that Olivia was as materialistic as they come.

"Okay, you got me there. Hey, listen, I need to grab one more bite and run. Holly needs to be taken out for a walk. Poor thing. She probably thinks I'm the worst dog mother in the world," Clara said.

"Somehow, I think she'll forget all about it as soon as she sees you walking through the door."

"I sure hope so."

"Hey, Clara. Keep me posted about Friday. I can't wait to hear how the saga unfolds. I can close my eyes and see the headlines now." Mackenzie pretended to be reading a newspaper.

"Clara Covington, the former housekeeper of Mrs. Joan Russell, inherits billions and leaves greedy family members groveling at her feet." She giggled.

"Will you lower your voice? I can't tell you anything. You're going to have these people running around thinking that really happened," Clara scolded.

"Hold on to your girdle. I'm just kidding around with ya. Even though, it would be nice if you inherited billions. I'm just saying."

Clara picked up the nearest newspaper and gave Mackenzie a friendly swat on the arm with it. Afterward, she took one last sip of her coffee, and then blew a kiss to her friend before heading out the door.

~

The following afternoon, Ms. Mae walked in with her cane in one hand and a slight limp. She checked the schedule hanging on a clipboard and cringed at the idea of only having one tour for the day. Clara returned to the front in time to hear her fussing aloud about it.

"Hey, Ms. Mae. Is everything all right?"

She waved her hand in disgust.

"Eh, everything will be fine after I get a hold of Mike and have a talk with him about this schedule. He's pampering me too much. Ever since I returned from my knee surgery, he's given me one tour a day and some days no tours at all. I'm sick of it. I didn't sign up for a desk job. No offense, Clara," she said.

"None taken. I'm sure it has to be an adjustment for you. God knows I've had my share of changes lately," Clara murmured.

Ms. Mae pulled up a chair a few feet behind Clara's desk and made herself comfortable. Clara wondered if the reason

Mike was limiting her tours was because she needed to sit and rest so often. She wouldn't dare say it out loud for fear it might upset Ms. Mae.

"So, what's your story? You sound like you've been going through a tough time," Ms. Mae asked Clara.

"Do I? I'm sorry. The last thing I want to do is to be a Debbie downer. It just seems like everything is changing as of late, and I guess I'm just trying to figure it all out," Clara responded.

"Honey, don't apologize. We've all been through life changes at some point or another. It doesn't matter that you're going through changes. What matters is where you end up, after all is said and done. I've been around here long enough to watch just about every one of these fellas go through something. I'm sure they'll share with you in due time, but Brody lost his business two years ago. He used to have his own mechanic shop until the finances went down the tubes. Jonathan had a major health scare last year. The doctors thought it was a terminal illness, but thankfully, further testing proved otherwise. And Mike, poor thing..." Ms. Mae folded her arms and shook her head.

"Mike lost the love of his life several years back. Like I said, every one of us has been through something. The good news is we all turned out all right in the end. The same will happen for you, I'm sure of it."

Clara wanted to press in and ask more about Mike's situation but thought better of it.

"Mind if I ask you a question?" Ms. Mae said.

"Not at all. Ask away."

"I promise I won't say anything, but do you like him?" she asked.

"I'm sorry?" Clara's forehead creased.

"Mike. Do you like like him? The two of you look like you

had a thing yesterday. You know, that little dance you were doing around each other. That's what happens when two people like each other. If you ask me, he sure is sweet on you," Ms. Mae whispered.

Clara's face turned flush. Just then, Mike returned from his lighthouse tour and startled Ms. Mae when he passed her by. She straightened up in her chair and immediately switched the subject.

"Hello, ladies," he said.

"Don't 'hello, ladies' me. I have a bone to pick with you, sir," Ms. Mae replied. Although he was the boss, she had no problem expressing herself however she saw fit. It was the kind of thing that could only come from many years of working together. That, plus Mike had a healthy level of respect for his elders.

"Uh, oh. What did I do now, Ms. Mae?" Mike groaned.

"What's with you giving me one tour again today? I need to get back out there and work, Mike. If the doctor didn't give me orders to stay off my knee completely, then why are you punishing me like this?" Ms. Mae stared him right in the eye and waited for a response.

"Come on, ease up a little. You just got out of surgery. Don't you think it would be wise to ease into your old schedule, rather than diving in full speed ahead? By the time summer hits, we'll be in full swing and I'll really need you then. If we overwork that knee now, you'll be out of commission again. Need I remind you what you felt like prior to surgery?" he asked.

"No... you need not remind me of anything. If doc approved my return, then you can add at least one more tour to my schedule." Mae pouted and then left him with a final thought.

"I won't take no for an answer, boss. Sorry, but I've never

been one for pushing papers across a desk, and I'm not about to start now." Ms. Mae exited the room and Mike let out a deep sigh.

"Looks like she means business," Clara said.

"She always means business. Technically, I'm her superior, but in reality, she's the boss." He laughed. "Gotta love her, though. We've been working together for a mighty long time. She followed me here from the Annapolis office. She's been with me through everything, so as long as it's within reason, I let her do her own thing. She just likes to keep busy, that's all. If you ask me, I think she's afraid of slowing down and aging too quickly."

"We all age. It's a natural part of life," Clara said.

"Yeah, well, try telling that to Ms. Mae." He laughed.

The room fell into an awkward period of silence. Clara returned to her desk to make it seem like she was busy, but the truth was the afternoon was quiet and she had little to do.

"Hey, Mike. I'm almost done with my to-do list. Now might be the perfect time for me to learn something new, if you have the time to teach me," she said.

Mike glanced at the schedule, which was pretty wide open for the afternoon. He checked his watch and then his face lit up with the biggest smile.

"I have the perfect plan. I don't know why I didn't think of this before now. The best way for you to get on-the-job training is to take a personalized tour with me," he said.

"Wait, say what now? You want me to go on the boat with you?"

"Yeah, I figured I could give you the experience of what we offer from the customer's point of view. Unless you're uncomfortable. Jonathan is out back. I could always ask him or Ms. Mae to join us," Mike said.

"It's not that."

"Well, what is it? Do you suffer from motion sickness?" he asked.

"No, I mean. I don't know, honestly. I'm kind of embarrassed to admit this, but I've never been on a boat before," Clara admitted.

"Never?"

"Not really. I know that's unheard of living out here where you are surrounded by so much water, but the closest I ever get to water is by visiting the beach on foot. And, sadly, even that has dwindled down to the bottom of my list as of late," she said.

"We have to do something about this immediately. This is like a state of emergency or something close to it. We can't have you living on the island without having at least one experience on a boat." Mike raised the side of his mouth with the cutest smile.

"Now, grab your things. I'm about to give you the first and best nautical experience you've ever had," he said with confidence.

"Where are we going?"

"The lighthouse, of course. Where else? Hello. Did you forget I'm the captain of the lighthouse tours already? It's only day two, and you're already slipping on the job," he teased.

"Right, the lighthouse, how could I forget?"

Clara grabbed a light jacket and followed Mike to the dock out back. On the way outside they passed Ms. Mae, who was watching them rather suspiciously.

"Ms. Mae, hold down the fort for me. I'm going to give Clara some on-the-job training. We should be back in a couple of hours," he yelled.

She waved Mike on to confirm that she heard everything he said.

"Mmm hmm, I got your on-the-job training, all right. Is that what these young kids are calling it these days?" she mumbled.

Jonathan overheard Ms. Mae and burst out in uncontrollable laughter.

"Behave yourself, Mae. Don't go stirring up trouble," he warned.

"Jonathan, you know me very well by now. There's absolutely nothing wrong with stirring up good trouble. Besides, the boss has a thing for the new assistant, and you and I both know it."

He laughed again.

"Hey, leave me out of this. I like my job and I plan on keeping it. Maybe if you weren't so focused on Mike, you'd notice me trying to give you a little attention."

Jonathan cranked the engine of his boat and winked at her while steering his way out of the dock. He tipped his hat at her and took off before she had time to respond. Prior to now, Ms. Mae was too fixated on the lives of others to notice that she may have an admirer of her own.

"Well, I'll be damned. Didn't see that one coming," she said to herself.

CHAPTER 9

"Okay, first things first. In order for you to truly appreciate this tour and learn something, you should probably open your eyes," Mike said. He found humor in watching Clara clench her fists and squeeze her eyes shut.

She tried to inhale the fresh air but found herself wanting to puke everything she ate that morning.

"I'm sorry. I'm doing the best I can, but being out here on the water is making me feel a little queasy."

"Oh, man. You look like you're turning three shades of green. I have to keep my hands on the wheel, but I have a few things that might help you. Reach inside that cabinet over there and grab a Dramamine and a bottle of water. That should fix you right up."

Clara clenched her teeth to keep from gagging and did as Mike instructed. Toward the front, Mike sat in the captain's chair and maneuvered the boat just like it was second nature to him. She caught a glimpse of the wind blowing in his hair and a tan on the back of his neck.

"Are you all right back there?" he yelled.

"I think I'll be okay. Just a little nauseous, that's all."

"We're just a mile out from the lighthouse. I'll share a little history with you to help take your mind off the nausea," he offered.

"The lighthouse was used in the eighteen hundreds to guide vessels along the shore of Chesapeake Bay. We usually stop at Drum Point Lighthouse first, and then make our way to Cove Point before heading back. The tourists absolutely love it."

"It sounds nice for those who have stomachs made of steel," Clara said.

"Eh, come on, you got this. Maybe you just need to build up your stamina. Take a few tours back and forth, and you'll be good in no time."

"Easier said than done. I think I'll be sticking to my desk job after today," Clara said in the most sincere tone she could muster up. *I'd much rather lay out on the beach and stick my feet in the water*, she thought to herself.

"So, do you normally give personal tours to your new employees?" she asked.

"Not really. You're the first newbie we've had in a long time, and hopefully the last for a while to come. We have a pretty tight-knit circle that works well together. I'd like to keep it that way, if you know what I mean," he responded.

"Makes sense. If you don't mind me asking, what led you to the boat tours industry?"

Mike slowed down as he reached the dock for their first stop.

"Wish I had a fancy answer for you, but it was the next best thing to get into after leaving the Coast Guard. When my partner approached me with the opportunity, I jumped on it. It gave me an opportunity to reconnect with being at sea again. Well, not exactly the sea, but you get the idea." He smiled.

"Yeah, I do. That's pretty neat, Mike. Why did you end up leaving the Coast Guard? That sounds like such an awesome way to serve our country," she asked.

"It would take much longer than a boat ride to the lighthouse to tell that story. But, the short version is I was released on an honorable discharge. I guess you could say I went through a traumatic experience that was a bit tough to bounce back from at the time. I came around eventually."

His voice trailed off into a moment of awkward silence.

"Now, enough about me." Mike secured the boat and walked to the back to extend his hand to Clara.

"Let me help you get your footing here." He helped her out of the boat and grabbed another bottle of water for her.

"You're starting to look better already, but I'll throw an extra bottle in my backpack just in case," Mike said.

In that moment, Clara recognized a desire and curiosity to know more about Mike. *What am I thinking?* she asked herself. "This guy is my boss and even if it feels like a date, it's not one. Get it together, Clara. Has it been that long since you've been with a man that you could be so desperate?" She shook her head in disgust and furrowed her brow.

Mike turned around and caught Clara in mid-thought.

"Are you all right?" he asked.

"If you're still feeling that bad, we can head back and do this some other time," Mike offered.

"No, no. Please, we're here now," she reassured him.

Mike led Clara along the dock and began giving her a personalized tour.

"If you look from this angle, you can see how the water opens up into the Chesapeake Bay." He positioned her to see the area he was pointing to.

"What a tranquil view. This place is so peaceful I feel like I could stand here forever." Clara closed her eyes and soaked in the sun's warmth.

When she opened her eyes, Mike was towering slightly above admiring her, or at least she thought he was.

He quickly shifted gears, cleared his throat, and pointed toward a building.

"Over there you have the marine museum, which is always a popular request among our clients as well."

"I'll bet. It looks like you could spend hours exploring out here and still not see it all. I'm grateful for the tour. This way when people call to book an appointment, I can do a better job at selling the experience," Clara said.

"Now, we're talking. That was the whole point of giving you this experience. I'd love for you to experience Ms. Mae's dinner tour, and Jonathan's fishing tour as well. We might have to give you a virtual experience so you can avoid all the nausea," Mike offered.

"Or, perhaps I can take a dose of that medicine you gave me prior to going on the boat. There has to be a way to conquer this thing, right?"

Mike smiled and nodded in agreement with Clara. He appeared to enjoy her enthusiasm and her go-getter mentality. She sensed that if they had met under different circumstances, he may have enjoyed getting to know her personally. It's too bad she would never know. In some ways it made her wonder if their encounter the night of the accident was fate leading her to new employment, or if it was a missed opportunity for something else.

"Yes, you've definitely proven that if you really want something, you go after it and make it happen, Clara. I like that spirit. It will serve you well in life," he said.

"How did I prove that to you? Technically, we've only known each other for what... a little over a week."

"Think about it. All I had to do was mention that we were hiring. You knew little about it, but you marched right in here the next morning to claim the position," he said.

"Makes sense. I do have a way of diving in and making things happen if the situation calls for it. I guess it's that same mentality that brought me here to Maryland in the first place." She regretted the moment the words slipped out, assuming that Mike would want to know more.

"Please, do tell," Mike asked.

"Eh, there's not much to it, really."

"Wait a minute, that's not how this works. I shared a little about my background. Now it's your turn. I took Mackenzie's word about you, but it would be nice to know more about you other than you were a former housekeeper," he said.

"Touché. Okay, where do I begin? Like yourself it would take more than a boat ride to get into all the details, but in a nutshell, I came to Maryland thinking that I needed a mini vacation. A little get away if you will. Turns out, I was really searching for a fresh start in life. When I found it, I never returned home. At least, I never returned there to live. I have been back occasionally to take care of family business, but that's about it."

"Where's home for you?" he asked.

"New York. My sister is the only surviving family member back home, and let's just say we don't really talk much."

"Say no more. I understand," he responded.

"Do you have siblings?"

"No, but you don't need one to understand that family relationships can be tricky at times," he said.

"Amen to that."

Back at the boat, Mike assisted Clara aboard and handed her the same life jacket she wore on the way there.

"As soon as you're all fastened up, I'll pull this baby out of here so we can get back before your meds wear off." He chuckled.

"Aw, crap. I wasn't even thinking about it. Thanks for the reminder," she teased.

"Don't worry, I'm sure the waves will remind you."

"Great, thanks," Clara said.

"No problem, that's what I'm here for." He continued to poke fun.

"I keep meaning to ask about your headlamp. How did the repairs turn out?"

"It looks as good as new. By the way, Al said he expects to see you in the shop soon. He said you don't have to worry about the cost. He's happy to work with his long-standing customers," Mike said.

"He's the best. I'll have to go by there soon. I'm about due for an oil change, anyway," Clara bent over trying to ward off that icky feeling that was rising with every bump and splash in the boat.

"Ah, don't you just love that fresh air," he asked.

"Mmm hmm," she moaned.

What should've been a quick ride felt like an eternity. All Clara wanted to do was make it back without hurling in front of Mike. She was intent on sitting still and trying to maintain control until they made it back to shore.

～

"Hello," the sound of a five-year-old voice answered on the other end of the line.

"Hi, Stephanie. It's Ms. Clara. How are you, sweetheart?"

"I'm good. Would you like to talk to Mommy?"

"I'd love to talk to her if she's not too busy," Clara said.

"Okay, I'll go get her for you."

In the background, Clara could hear Mackenzie pleading with her little girl to clean up and get ready for bed. She didn't know how Mackenzie did it, but she worked tirelessly during the day and gave her all to provide little Stephanie the best life she could as a single mother. Stephanie's father was a deadbeat dad who made occasional appearances a few times a year. His priorities were on the road with his traveling band and dreams of making it big someday.

"Hey, Clara," Mackenzie said.

"Hey, you sound exhausted. Is this a bad time?" Clara asked.

"No, you're good. I just finished running a nice hot bath, and I plan on putting my hair up and soaking in the tub, girl. It's the perfect time to catch up. How's the new job coming along?"

"It's..." Clara hesitated. "It's coming along fine, I guess," she said.

"Uh, oh. What's the matter? Do you miss your house-keeping gig?"

"No, surprisingly, I like the challenge of trying something completely different. It's not that at all," Clara said.

"Then, what is it? Why the hesitation?"

"First, you need to promise me you will take what I'm about to say seriously and you won't tease," Clara pleaded.

"Oh, this is going to be good, whatever it is." Mack chuckled.

"Mack! I'm being serious."

"All right, I won't poke fun. Whenever I do, you know it's all in love, anyway. Now, tell me what's on your mind, kiddo," Mack said.

After a long pause, Clara took a deep breath and revealed her secret.

"I think I made a mistake by taking this job. I mean... God

knows I needed to get my act together fast, and I definitely needed the money. But, maybe I was hasty to accept a job working with Mike," she confessed.

"What? Clara, why would you say a thing like that? I thought you liked the challenge of trying something new?"

"I do. Everything about the job is perfect, except..."

"Except what?" Mackenzie asked.

"How can I continue working there if I'm attracted to my boss? I don't know what's gotten into me, but I feel like an animal that's been released into the wild. I guess this is what I get for putting dating off for so long. I thought the guy was kind of cute right from the start. But, I was willing to put those thoughts aside because I desperately needed the job. The thing is, I probably could ignore my feelings, but..." Clara lowered her voice. "I think he's into me, too. And, even if I thought I was imagining things, I know Ms. Mae isn't. She made that rather clear earlier today," Clara said.

"Didn't I tell you getting that job was a sign? Man, this is better than catching up on my daytime soaps recorded on my DVR." Mackenzie couldn't help but poke a little fun, even though she promised not to.

"Mack!"

"All right, all right, no teasing. Got it. I'm inclined to believe that you are not hallucinating if Ms. Mae thinks there's something going on. That woman is as sharp as they come. But, how did all of this come about? Mike always presents himself like a gentleman when he comes to the café. Is he coming on to you at the job?" Mackenzie asked.

"No, not at all. I can't explain it. It's the subtle little things that guys do when they're into somebody. You know."

"Like?" Mackenzie pressed further.

"Like awkwardly getting in the way when I'm trying to get to my chair and then fumbling over himself to the point of embarrassment. Or gazing at me from across the room and staring with a lingering smile until something snaps him out of it. It sounds silly, I know. But it's real, and it's happening whenever we interact with each other. He's being the ultimate professional. But, I look forward to getting to work early in the morning, and I'm wondering if it's for all the wrong reasons."

"I told you. I knew he was a good catch from the start," Mackenzie proudly declared.

"I'm sure he is a good catch for somebody, but he's my boss. I have to rein it in now before this gets out of hand. You should've seen me earlier today when he took me out to the lighthouse. I wanted our time out there to last so I could get to know him more. He told me the story of his honorable discharge from the Coast Guard. Apparently, there was some sort of traumatic event that caused him to leave. All I wanted to do was sit and listen. In a perfect world where we didn't work together, the outing today could've easily been a date. The fact that I look at him that way can only mean trouble if I'm not careful going forward," Clara said.

"Okay, so you're human. Those hormones of yours still work after several years of celibacy. Give yourself a break. You did nothing wrong, and there's no reason to question whether this is the job for you. I say be a professional by day and whatever happens after hours is up to your discretion. You probably need a little nighttime action to help calm down those hormones, anyway." Mackenzie laughed.

"Mack, come on. Get real. That's not a good idea and you know it."

"Give me a break. Everybody in this town is married to somebody I know, related to somebody I know, interested in somebody I know, or shacking up with somebody I know. Take Jonathan, for example. Did you know he's been pursuing Ms.

Mae for months now? She doesn't have a clue," Mackenzie said.

"No, I didn't know."

"Mmm hmm, well he is. But if you tell him I said so, I'll deny it. Oh, and the mystery of Mike's honorable discharge is actually rather tragic. I don't know all the details, but it's my understanding he witnessed his fiancé being killed while they were both serving together," Mackenzie admitted.

"Oh, man. That's terrible."

"Tell me about it," Mack said.

"Hey, how do you know all this? What are you, like, the town mayor or something?"

"No, I'm not the mayor, but I do work at the café, aka gossip central. Even though a lot of it I hear firsthand. Some of it I overhear, but you know, it's all the same thing." She giggled.

"Yeah, sure, if you say so," Clara said.

"So, what are you going to do?"

"Well, now that I've talked things out, which feels very therapeutic, by the way, I'm not going to do anything but lie here with Holly, get a good night's rest, and wake up refreshed and ready to be the ultimate professional in the morning. I'm lucky to even have a job so soon given my situation. The last thing I want to do is mess things up," Clara said.

"I guess that's an acceptable plan for now. The jury is still out on what the future may hold. In the meantime, you still need to work on getting out there and explore the dating scene again."

"Oh, God, no. I can't do it. If I can't meet a guy in some sort of natural and authentic way, then I'll just accept living alone for the rest of my life. I wasn't built for dating apps, online dating, matchmaking, and whatnot. I get irritated just thinking about it," Clara said.

Mackenzie sighed on her end of the line.

"What is he supposed to do? Fall out of the sky and into your lap?" Mackenzie asked.

"Perhaps, but I'm not worried about it. That's up to him to figure out."

"You're such a nut job, but I love you just the same, girl," Mackenzie said.

"Love ya."

CHAPTER 10

*M*ike emerged from his office with receipts in hand and a look of frustration. As he marched over to the coffee machine, he let out a sigh. He was a creature of habit, and it was becoming obvious to Clara whenever he was in the midst of a problem he couldn't solve. His frustrations usually began with pacing, it may include a few sighs, and it always ended up at the coffee machine.

"Having a hard time?" She slowly spun around in her office chair.

"Is it that obvious?" he asked.

"Let's put it this way. I haven't been working here long, but I'm pretty good at picking up on body language. Something has you in a tizzy."

"Ha, you're right. I never learned how to develop a poker face," he said before taking a sip of coffee. "My dad used to always tell me to stop wearing my feelings on my sleeve. Guess I never mastered that one."

"Well, what's bothering you? Maybe I can help," Clara offered.

"Nah, it's fine. Your day is about to conclude in a few minutes. I'd hate to hold you up with something so ridiculous. Besides, I'm sure you have somebody waiting for you to come home... I would imagine."

"Yes, I have a companion," Clara said.

"Oh, what's the lucky guy's name?"

Clara giggled, which caused Mike to look at her with a puzzled smirk on his face.

"Her name is Holly. She's my newly adopted canine. Thankfully, I found a sweet teenager in the building who walks the dogs in the neighborhood, so Holly should be fine."

"Oh, Holly, your dog. Right. Sorry, I don't know why I assumed you were talking about..."

His voice trailed off.

"A guy?" she said.

"Well, yeah. I just figured a woman like yourself would probably be taken, that's all."

"Hardly!" Clara responded with so much emphasis she had to reconsider how it may have sounded.

"It's not that I wouldn't mind having a male companion, I just haven't met the right one. Sorry, that's probably TMI," she said.

"No, don't apologize. I get it. It's difficult getting out there and meeting new people. Especially in this day and age. All this modern technology has replaced human interaction. It's crazy. That's why I love it out here on the Island. People out here believe in face-to-face communication; they know each other by name. Most of the folks out here grew up in the area, went to school together, and started families of their own right here in Solomons Island," Mike said.

"Do you like it here even better than Annapolis?"

"Annapolis is beautiful, too. But, in a different way. Out

here, it's quiet. It's peaceful. I can count the stars at night. If I ever miss Annapolis, it's just a boat ride away," he said.

Forgetting he was in the midst of a problem he was trying to solve, Mike glanced down at the receipts in his hand.

"So, what are you trying to figure out?" Clara asked.

"Well, I was trying to go through some of Brody's expenses and identify a few loopholes. I have about four months of receipts here and everything is all disorganized. It's all my fault. I swore at the beginning of the year I was going to do a better job at keeping track of this stuff, but so far I haven't made a lick of progress," he said.

"I can totally help with that. I mean, you'll still be in charge of figuring out the numbers, but I was born to organize things. I don't see why this would be any different."

"You're sure? It's four o'clock. I can always try to tackle round two with Brody when he comes in later this week," Mike said.

"Let me at least try to take a stab at it. It may not be much, but if you lead me to all your receipts, I'll put them in order by date and by month. That way, you can readily identify what's missing and check the amounts without taking forever to find what you're looking for," Clara said.

"All right, but before we step inside my office, I should warn you it looks like a war zone. You might be sorry you volunteered to help after you see what's on the other side of this door."

The door to Mike's office creaked open to an unsightly view of stacks of receipts spread out everywhere.

"Good God," Clara said.

"I thought you said there were four months' of receipts? This looks more like a year's worth. And this is just from Brody's expenses?" She continued.

"Well, I'm looking for Brody's expenses amid all the others."

"Goodness. I hope we don't find any living creatures underneath one of these piles in here." Clara was grossed out and didn't mind letting it be known.

"Tell me how you really feel. I tried to warn ya." Mike laughed.

"I'm sorry. I just don't know how you can think straight in an atmosphere like this. The good news is you hired the right girl for the job. We're gonna whip these receipts into place in no time. Then afterward, we're going to get you signed up for one of those receipt tracking apps or something like it," she said.

"No, ma'am. I'm as old school as they come. I've already agreed to start one of those new techy programs this month, and that's already more than I can stand."

Two hours and several organized piles later, Clara had everything sorted by the months of the year and by various vendors. She twisted her hair up in a bun to make herself comfortable and took off her heels so she could comfortably spread out on the floor to position her stacks. Mike was on all fours beside her, watching intently as he learned her system.

"Okay, there you have it. You should be able to start with the January pile over here. If you take this stack to your computer, everything you need to know is sorted by vendor and date. Whatever you do, don't remove the paperclips until you're ready to go through the piles."

Her stomach growled obnoxiously, which interrupted her thought and made both of them laugh.

"And, that's our signal to stop while we're ahead," Mike said.

"Clara, this is amazing. I would've still been here sorting through everything if it hadn't been for your high level of organization. But I feel terrible. It's six o'clock, two hours past the end of your shift, and you're starving." He continued.

Clara waved her hand as if she was dismissing the extra effort put into helping him.

"No, seriously. It's not your job to put in overtime hours. I don't want you to think I'm going to be in the habit of keeping you after work."

"It's nothing, really. I don't mind helping out. Especially with something like this. Blame it on my former line of work, but organizing is a strong suit for me," she said with a smile.

"At least let me send you home with a hot meal from the café. We can put in an order with Mackenzie. I'm sure they have something good on the specials menu for tonight."

"You really don't..." Clara began to protest, but Mike interrupted.

"I want to. Besides, I'm dining at the front counter tonight, and the place is only a few feet away. I've never met anybody who passed up a free meal from the café. Don't tell me you're going to be the first."

"Okay, you win," Clara said as she slid her feet back into her heels.

"How about you give me five minutes to freshen up, and I'll meet you out front," she said.

"Sounds good."

∼

Mackenzie tucked her pen at the top of her ear and folded her arms with an expression of disbelief smeared across her face. Clara figured the sight of her and Mike walking in together would get a rise out of Mack, but she didn't expect that much of a reaction. *Under normal circumstances, what was the big deal with grabbing a bite to go with your boss?* Clara thought to herself.

"Well, well. What do we have here? Two of my favorite people dining together. Come on in and pull up a chair," Mack said.

"Oh, we're not dining together. We're just making a quick pit stop to take something to go," Clara said.

Mike nodded in agreement and waved hello to Mackenzie.

"Yeah, Clara has to get home to her dog, and I probably need to go back to the office for at least another hour," Mike said.

"That's ridiculous. The two of you need to sit down and eat your meal while it's nice and hot. Clara... Mike... have a seat right here at my station. I need some company, anyway. Josh is about to drive me crazy tonight. If I hear one more story about this restoration project he's working on, I'm gonna lose it," she complained.

Josh was standing within earshot and heard everything. He refrained from making a comment but stuck out his tongue at Mackenzie while escorting customers to their table. They were work buddies, so it was kind of hard not to talk about every aspect of their lives in between serving customers.

"Hey, that sounds neat. What is he restoring?" Mike asked.

"A vintage car of some sort. He's been ordering car parts for weeks. One minute he watches a few shows about car restoration, and the next thing I know, he's an expert. God help us all when he finally puts this thing on the road." Mackenzie laughed.

"Enough about that. What can I get you to drink?" She continued.

Clara darted her eyes at Mackenzie for seating them against her wishes. Of course, Mack being who she was, totally ignored Clara and positioned her pen to take down their order.

"Ladies first," Mike said.

"Thanks, I'll have a Coke and a hot open turkey sandwich. It may be spring, but the evenings are still chilly if you ask me." Clara rubbed the goosebumps on her arms.

"It sure is chilly this evening. That hot open turkey sandwich will warm you right up. You having your usual cheesecake tonight?" Mack asked.

"I think I'll pass. My poor waistline is going to look like cheesecake if I don't start exercising some restraint."

The ladies joked about their ongoing battles with desserts and waistlines. But the entire time Mike looked at Clara with an innocent smile. When the laughter died down, he finally broke his silence.

"You shouldn't say that about yourself. You look great just the way you are," he said. Then, he looked at Mackenzie and added, "You both look great. I wouldn't change a thing about either of you."

Mackenzie winked at Clara. It was her subtle acknowledgement of everything they talked about on the phone last night.

"Mike, you can come hang out in my section of the café any day of the week. Now, what can I get for you tonight? After a late night at the office, I know you have to be hungry," Mack said.

"I think I'll give the hot open turkey sandwich a try with a side of fries. Oh, and I'll take a beer, please."

"All righty. One beer, a Coke, two hot open turkeys, and a side of fries coming right up. I'll be right back." Mack disappeared through the kitchen doors to place their order.

Across the café, a local group of women were grumbling over a game of Parcheesi. It wasn't uncommon to see people hanging around for a few hours indulging in hobbies they shared in common.

"So. Give me your honest opinion. I know you haven't been working with us very long, but what are your thoughts about working at the Lighthouse so far? And, don't be shy about it. Pretend you're not talking to your boss right now. Give it to me straight," Mike said.

"Well, thankfully, I have nothing bad to say or else this would be awkward. But, so far, so good. I like working at Lighthouse Tours." Clara smiled.

"Yeah?"

"Yes, you sound surprised. What's not to like? I love scheduling tours, the clients are amazing, and Ms. Mae is absolutely hilarious. That woman keeps me entertained, for sure," Clara said.

Mike's eyes crinkled at the corners as he sat back and laughed.

"She's something, isn't she?" he said.

"She sure is. Then there's Jonathan and Brody. I'm still getting to know them, but they've been great so far. Everyone has welcomed me and made me feel like an instant member of the team. Actually, more like a member of the work family."

"That warms my heart. I've always stressed to my employees how important it is to stick together and create a great work environment for each other. I'm glad that's been your experience so far," Mike said.

Mackenzie served their drinks and leaned over to share a little café humor with them.

"You two want to see something funny? Once I walk away, turn around and check out old Bobby sitting at the corner table by the window. It never fails. Every evening by seven he's as drunk as a skunk and falls asleep sitting upright with his mouth cocked open. I don't know how many times I thought about pouring some Tabasco sauce in his mouth just to get a rise out of him." Mackenzie cracked herself up on the way back to the kitchen.

"You wouldn't dare," Clara yelled.

They peeked over at Bobby and chuckled.

"Hey, at least he's in here minding his business and not bothering anybody," Mike said.

"That's true."

After a quiet moment passed, Clara decided to loosen up and enjoy getting to know Mike.

"Okay, so now it's my turn. I want to ask you a similar question," she said.

"Uh, oh."

"Don't worry. It won't be painful. I just want to know what you think of me as your new employee. Am I turning out to be the assistant you hoped I would be or..." She hesitated.

"Aw, definitely. Anybody can learn the inner workings of the job, but it takes the right personality to handle the customer service aspect, to work well with others, and to keep me in line when I get disorganized. You're definitely an asset to us," Mike said.

"Good."

"So, enough about work. Tell me more about yourself. What do you like to do during your downtime?" he asked.

"Sadly, I have nothing exciting to report. I spend most of my evenings hanging out with Holly and organizing the last few boxes that need to be unpacked. I'm usually so exhausted these days that I end up conking out before the nightly news comes on," Clara confessed.

"Yeah, but surely you'll get back to doing something for fun once you're officially settled in."

"Fun? What's that? I come here and hang out with Mack when I feel like getting out. That's about as fun as it gets," Clara responded.

"Wait. How long have you been living here again?"

"Ten years, but you have to keep in mind that I'm a home-body at heart, plus I was a live-in housekeeper and good friends with my boss before she passed away. Even when she got sick, I willingly stayed home and took care of her. I know it sounds kind of strange that I haven't explored around more. I guess I must add that to my to-do list," she said.

"Let me start by offering my condolences. Your boss must've meant a lot to you. It says a lot about your character that you would be there for her when she was sick. Now it makes even more sense to me that she would leave you in her will. It sounds like you were a true gem in her eyes."

"Thank you, Mike," Clara responded.

"I also want to officially extend an invitation to be your tour guide to the area."

"What? No... no." She refused.

"Yeah, why not? It makes perfect sense. You desperately need to get out and learn more about this town you call home. And, I just happen to be the ultimate tour guide. It's a win-win situation. I get to revisit some well-known places here in the area, and you receive a personal tour free of charge."

"Mike, I can't put you out of your way like that."

"Why not? We'll go after hours, of course. Come on. I promise to keep you on dry land this time," he offered.

Just then Mackenzie returned to the table with their food. The fresh aroma of hot open turkey sandwiches was enough to make anybody's stomach rumble with delight.

"Hey, Mackenzie, will you talk to your girl over here? Tell her it's about time that she gets out and explores Solomons Island, instead of staying home all the time. I offered to give her a tour, but she won't budge," Mike said.

"Sorry, Clara. I'm with Mike on this one. You do need to get out more. People pay good money to go on his tours, so if he's offering, I wouldn't refuse. Now, here are your fries and a few napkins. I'm going to check on a few customers. Holler for me if you need anything." Mack left just as quickly as she arrived. Normally, she'd sit down and spend time with Clara, so her frequent disappearing acts didn't go unnoticed and appeared to be intentional.

"See, even Mackenzie is backing me on this one. Your first official tour can start as early as this Saturday at nine a.m. You should wear a pair of hiking shoes and come dressed to explore the great outdoors. And, by all means, bring a friend along if it will make you feel more comfortable. What do you say?"

In a soft-spoken voice Clara asked, "Are you sure?"

"I wouldn't offer if I wasn't. Think of it as an investment. The more you know about the area, the more you can talk up our tours." He smiled.

"That sounds like a good proposition to me. Count me in." Clara extended her hand across the table to seal the deal.

∾

With a full belly, Clara grew comfortable in her chair and didn't want to leave. The conversation with Mike was pleasant but, with Holly on her conscience, she knew it was best to get going. They said their goodbyes to Mackenzie and took a slow stroll out to Clara's car, which was parked inches away from the space where they first met.

"I'm right over here," she said.

"Trust me, I remember your car very well. I can still close my eyes and hear the crunching sound of your bumper doing the tango with my headlamp."

"Let me guess. You plan on holding that against me from now until eternity, don't you?" Clara laughed.

"Not true. But, I do plan on teasing you about it for a while longer. I gotta have a little fun first, you see. Then, I'll let it go maybe five or ten years down the line," he said.

"Oh, I see. So, you plan on keeping me around the Lighthouse company for at least five to ten years, just so you can tease me. That's good to know." Clara poked right back at him.

She walked around to the driver's side and clicked her remote control to unlock the doors. Mike followed her and held the door open as only a gentleman would. Once inside, she put the window down. He bent over slightly to say his goodbyes.

"All right, how about this. I'll only tease you about the car one or two more times. Maybe three times max. But, we'll keep you here at the Lighthouse for as long as you'd like a position with us. How does that sound?" Mike asked.

Clara looked at him and revealed all her pearly white teeth before responding.

"Hey, I'm tough, so I can deal with a little teasing, that's nothing. And, there's nothing like job security, so I'm good with that, too."

"Well, all right, then. We'll see you in the morning. Thanks again for your help this evening. Drive safe now." Mike tapped the hood of the car and walked across the street toward the Lighthouse Tours company. Watching him gave her this warm, fuzzy feeling on the inside. She didn't want to make much of it, but she was also having a hard time ignoring it.

CHAPTER 11

*C*lara stood in the supply room searching for brochures for the front desk. She was startled by hands that embraced her waist from behind and a sensual voice that softly whispered, "I have a surprise for you. Turn around slowly." She tried her best to turn but it felt like no matter what she did, it was a struggle. Finally, she rolled over to the sound of her favorite radio station blaring today's weather. The gentle hands that felt so real and the man's voice no longer existed. Sadly, it was all a dream. Clara was agitated. Instead of seeing the face of the man in her dreams, all she was left with was the weather report from her alarm clock. "It's going to be a high of sixty-eight with clear skies today."

"Ugh," Clara moaned.

She stretched as far as her arm could reach to slap the snooze button. But after three attempts, it was time to emerge from the sheets and take Holly outside.

After her usual cup of oatmeal with raisins, she skimmed the closet for something to wear to work. With a tight budget she was already recycling outfits and mix-matching whenever she could. Eventually, she would have to give in and purchase a few new outfits against her will.

"Holly, what do you think, sweet girl? Should I wear the navy-blue pants with the white blouse? Or should I repeat the black dress?"

Holly watched Clara with her tail wagging. She took that as a sign of approval for the navy-blue pants.

On the drive in, her Bluetooth announced a call from an unknown number.

"Hello?"

"Clara?" the voice on the other end of the line said.

"Yes, who's speaking?"

"It's Olivia. If you have a minute we need to talk," she said.

"I have a few minutes to spare. How can I help you, Olivia?"

"I really wish you wouldn't play dumb with me. You know why I'm calling."

"Look," Clara said.

"No, you look. I think we can agree that my aunt was more than generous to you. My brother and I have been looking over her records. With the salary she paid you, plus the free room and board, you earned way more than what an average house-keeper would make. One might say that you were intentionally taking advantage," Olivia implied.

"What?"

"Save the innocent act," Olivia said with a sharp tone.

Clara was fuming but paid careful attention not to do anything irrational on the road. She continued to listen.

"Just know this. We will pursue you to the ends of the earth if you even think about taking anything from our family. Every-thing that's in that will belongs to Aunt Joan's blood relatives. Do I make myself clear?" Olivia asked.

Clara reached for the appropriate button and disconnected

the call. She had the mindset to drive straight to the police station and file a complaint. But, what would that accomplish? What was she going to complain about? Empty threats from a greedy woman? *Perhaps she should tell the lawyer what just happened*, she thought to herself. But, again, was she really afraid of Olivia? The whole thing was stupid. "This is exactly how people behave when greed dominates their very existence," she said out loud.

The phone rang one more time with the same unknown number. This time she sent the call straight to voicemail. With the push of a button, she turned on the radio and listened to something to help put her mind at ease before arriving to work.

∽

Around noon a woman with long blond hair, perky bosoms, and an hourglass figure walked in the front door of Lighthouse Tours. She immediately caught Brody's attention as she laid her purse and keys on the counter.

"How are you, Brody?" she asked.

"I'm doing well, Savannah. Looking for Mike?"

Clara tried to keep a straight face, but she could hardly believe what she was seeing. *Wasn't her top supposed to provide a little more coverage?* Clara thought to herself. *Was it supposed to be soo... see through?* she thought.

"I would like to see him if he's around," Savannah responded.

She glanced at Clara, sizing her up from head to toe before speaking.

"Well, hello there. You must be the new assistant. Aren't you a cutie," she said.

Savannah shook Clara's hand and made herself comfortable, leaning on one of the counters a few feet away from

Clara's desk. Clara didn't know who this woman was but figured she must be welcomed the way she was making herself feel right at home.

"Oh, don't worry. Everybody knows me very well around here."

"I see. Well, it's nice to meet you," Clara said.

"I don't recall Mike saying anything about finding a new assistant. How long have you been working here?"

"This is my first week," Clara responded.

"Oh, that's nice. How did you find out about the position?"

"It's a crazy story, really. Technically, Mike and I met when we got into a little fender bender. That was a whole scene. Totally my fault. But anyway, turns out we have a friend in common. She works across the street at the café, actually. Her name is Mackenzie. Do you know her?" Clara asked.

"I may have met her a time or two. I don't really hang out in places like that, though."

"Right. Well, he told me about the job, Mack put in a good word as one of my references. And, the rest, as they say, is history." Clara was trying to be friendly, but she didn't like the way Savannah was looking at her.

"Interesting. Mike must've been desperate. He normally makes his applicants go through a much more rigorous process than that," she said.

Clara clamped down on her bottom lip to keep from saying anything harsh. *This must be my lucky day,* she thought to herself. *First Olivia, and now this...* she thought.

"Savannah, hi. How can I help you?" Mike emerged from the back with one hand in his pocket and the other hand resting on a pen behind his ear.

"Well, hello to you, too, stranger. Why do you sound so professional?"

She placed her hand on his chest and nestled up close to give him a kiss on the cheek.

Mike glanced over at Clara and took a step back to continue talking to Savannah.

"Well, we are in my place of business. I didn't realize you were stopping by today. I'm kind of swamped with meetings this morning," Mike said.

"That's no problem. I'll let you get back to your meetings. I was wondering if you wanted to grab a bite to eat later on. Maybe you can stop by and we can have a little play date." She winked at him.

"Yeah, the thing is, I'm running the dinner tour this afternoon. By the time I'm done with that and then close up, it will probably be a late night," Mike responded. You could tell he felt uncomfortable, but somehow he was squirming his way through it.

Clara returned to her paperwork so she wouldn't seem nosey, but she was fully listening to the entire conversation.

"I guess you'll have to take a rain check, then. That's too bad. I was cooking up something very special for you tonight," Savannah said.

"I bet you were," Clara murmured ever so softly under her breath. She faked a cough and cleared her throat, leaving Brody in silent laughter while he continued filling out his paperwork on the other side of the room.

"We'll talk about it soon, but for now I really need to get back to my meeting," Mike said.

"All right. Fair enough." Clara heard the sound of lips smacking behind her before watching blondie pick up her belongings and storm out the front door.

Clara was thrilled to see Savannah go but even more thrilled to finally have a reason to stop thinking about Mike. Mixing business with pleasure always had the potential to be

MICHELE GILCREST

problematic if things didn't work out. She didn't want to end up like one of those hopeless women in the soap operas sleeping around with the boss.

"Clara, can I see you in my office for a minute?" Mike asked.

She had that feeling in the pit of her stomach like she was in hot water with the boss. He probably heard what she mumbled under her breath. *Dang it. You have to do a better job of controlling your tongue if you want to keep a job*, she thought to herself.

"Sure, Mike."

She got up and followed Mike to his office. Brody continued to find humor in the whole thing and sat grinning from ear to ear as Clara passed by. She jokingly stuck out her tongue at him.

Once behind closed doors Mike stood behind his desk.

"I owe you an apology for the way Savannah spoke to you. I heard her from the back. That wasn't right," he said.

Clara made light of it while internally breathing a sigh of relief.

"Eh, it was nothing. I'm a new face around here. Not everyone takes too kindly to having new people around," she said.

"Yeah, well, if everyone else can welcome you, she shouldn't be an exception to the rule."

"I'm sure she's just being protective," Clara suggested.

"Protective? Over what?"

"Uh, I don't mean to pry, but I would presume over you. Some women like to let it be known that their man is off limits," Clara said.

"But, we're not..." He stopped dead in his tracks. "We..." He just couldn't seem to find the right words to explain his complex situation.

"Never mind. Just know that it won't happen again. I vowed to create a work atmosphere where my employees are respected, and I plan to uphold that vow. I'll have a talk with her later, but I just wanted to make sure you know where I stand," he said.

"I appreciate that."

Mike looked at her with a longing in his eyes. It was as if he had so much more to say but couldn't due to the nature of their relationship.

"Hey, um, before you go. I have to take a few more telephone meetings, and then I'm heading out for the tour this afternoon. I just wanted to wish you good luck tomorrow morning in case I don't see you for the rest of the day. If there is such a thing. I really don't know what the right words are, but I wish you well," he said.

"Thanks, I'm actually going to need all the luck I can get. Joan's niece doesn't seem to be too thrilled with me. Even though I didn't do anything to deserve it."

"Let me guess, she sees you as some sort of threat?" he asked.

"Yeah, can you believe it? I'm sorry for doing my job and caring for the woman. Sorry that poses such a threat." Clara began pacing around the office.

"Maybe if she cared enough, she would've been more involved and wouldn't need to worry about anyone posing a threat. Anyone who really knows me also knows better," Clara said.

Mike watched as she slowly paced around.

"I'm sorry. I get fired up just talking about her. My day didn't exactly get off to the best start after receiving a call from her right before work. But, enough about that. You have another meeting to prepare for, and I need to get back up to the front desk," she said.

He glanced at the clock.

"I do have to get ready for this call, but I want to hear how things worked out when you get back tomorrow afternoon," he said.

Clara began walking toward the door.

"Thank you, but you didn't hire me to come here and talk about my drama," she said.

"Clara."

She turned around and made eye contact. He had one hand on the telephone as he leaned in to reiterate to her, "If I'm asking you, it's because I care. So, as long as you're comfortable sharing, I'd like to know."

"Sure," she said.

She whispered, "Have a good meeting," and backed slowly out of his office.

CHAPTER 12

"Mae, let's sit down and settle this thing once and for all. We can talk over lunch. Come on."

Jonathan pointed toward a bench several feet from the dock where they normally boarded the tours.

"What is there to settle?" she asked.

"Don't play innocent with me, Mae. We have some unfinished business to discuss. It feels like you've been dodging me ever since I revealed my feelings."

"I've done no such thing. I've just been busy, that's all."

"Busy? With what? All you've been doing is complaining about not having enough tours. How could you be busy? Now, are you going to come sit with me and give your knee a break or what?" he asked.

Ms. Mae followed Jonathan to the bench and proceeded to unzip her insulated lunch bag.

Jonathan popped open his cola, took a sip, and got straight to the point.

"So, what are you afraid of?" he asked.

"Pardon me?"

"You heard me, what are you afraid of, Anna Mae? You seem to enjoy my company, we make each other laugh, you call me whenever something urgent comes up, but the moment I reveal my feelings and start paying you extra attention, you start giving me the cold shoulder. I don't get it. Did I do something wrong?" Jonathan shrugged his shoulders.

Ms. Mae held her sandwich but didn't seem to have much of an appetite after hearing the sadness in Jonathan's voice. He was right. He had become a supportive friend over the years, a confidante. He was always there for her on a personal level. So why did she retreat at a time when he made himself so vulnerable?

"You haven't done anything wrong, Jonathan. You've done everything right. We've been friends, for what, almost eight years now?" she asked.

He nodded his head.

"You entered my life shortly after my Glynn died. You've seen me at my best and at the lowest point of my life. You were never just a co-worker, instead you became an instant friend, just when I needed you most," she said.

"Is that all you see me as? A friend and nothing more?"

"I have to be honest. I put you and every other man in that category and kept you there just because I don't know any other way. Glynn was my only lover. It may sound crazy but after he passed, I buried that part of my heart with him. I haven't made room in my life for another man since. It's not you, Jonathan. I promise, it's not you," she pleaded.

"So, just to be certain. You don't mind sharing meals with me, having me come to your aid, sharing long talks about life, getting to know each other's family members, but when it comes to the idea of becoming one, and falling in love, you have a problem with that?"

"I don't mean it like that, Jonathan," she said.

"Okay, well, here's how I mean it. I never expected to be more than a co-worker and friend to you, Mae. I swear I didn't. I knew that losing Glynn was probably one of the toughest things you had to go through. I also knew that it would take some time for your heart to heal. But, now, here it is eight years later, and I'm in love with you. I enjoy running by the house when you're sick to bring your favorite bowl of hot pea soup, and I enjoy our long talks. Not when the game is on, of course, but I do enjoy talking to you. And, I'm tired of going around pretending that we're just friends. Quite frankly, I don't know how you do it. It's like you're oblivious to what's really going on between us or you're simply not interested. Either way, I can't do this anymore. I love you, Anna Mae. Hell, I want to make love to you. I want the full package with you. But, if you don't want me in return, for the sake of sparing my heart, I have to make some serious changes. It's the only way. I have to move on," Jonathan said.

Mae stared at the veins in her hands. She felt an overwhelming sense of grief at the thought of losing Jonathan, yet she didn't know what to say.

"Somehow I figured this conversation would end in silence," Jonathan said.

"I'm going to give you some time to think about what I said. Whenever you're ready to talk, you know where to find me."

Jonathan watched a boat going by, hoping Mae would respond. When she didn't, he gathered his things, got up, and proceeded to walk away.

~

Mackenzie was dressed in all black when Clara stopped by the cafe. It was a part of the look that the new owner was going for, among other changes. Josh was serving his usual tables and there was a peppy new addition to the team named, Chloe.

A group of locals occupied the seats at the front counter, which was fine by Clara since she didn't plan to stay long.

"There she is. How's my girl doing?" Mackenzie asked.

"I'm beat. Thought I would pop my head in to say a quick hello before heading home," Clara said.

"Aww, that's too bad. You know I love it when you stay and keep me company."

"You didn't seem to care when I was in here with Mike the other night. I barely saw you that night," Clara responded.

"The two of you looked like you were having such a good conversation, I didn't want to interrupt, that's all."

"Mmm hmm," Clara grunted.

"So, tomorrow is the big day. Are you nervous?" Mackenzie asked.

"I just want to hurry up and get it over with. I hate to say it, but the less I have to interact with Olivia, the better off I'll be."

"I hear that," Mackenzie said.

"Hey, Mack, random question for you," Clara said.

"Sure, what's on your mind?"

"Did you know that Mike was dating someone? Tall, blond, lots of cleavage. I think her name is Savannah."

"Oh, God, help us all. Don't tell me she's back," Mackenzie complained.

In the midst of their conversation, Mack wiped down a few booths and put down fresh paper mats for the next set of customers.

"I know who she is. Around here, we lovingly refer to her as the town hoe bag when she's not standing within ear shot," Mack admitted.

"Man, I hope you don't talk about me like that when I'm not around." Clara laughed.

"Clara, come on. First of all, it's just a running joke between me and Josh, but you don't come close to carrying yourself like that woman and you know it. I don't know what he sees in her," Mack said.

"Really? You don't know what he sees in her? Try starting with those double D's.

They're enough to get anybody's attention."

"Yes, but besides that. She lacks personality, kindness, class, and she thinks the people who come to the café are beneath her."

"I guess in her eyes, Mike is an exception to the rule?" Clara asked.

"Girl, he's good looking, so he doesn't count. Listen, I don't know the woman very well, but I don't like what I see. The few times she's walked into this family-friendly environment she looked like she was dressed for the strip club. That coupled with the snotty attitude was enough to make me write her off. He can do better. Way better. Somebody like yourself would be more his speed. And, from the way he was looking at you the other night, I think he agrees." Mackenzie winked at Clara.

"Don't go planting ideas in my head," Clara said in a low voice. "He's my boss, remember?"

"I remember. That doesn't negate the fact that there's a little attraction thing going on between the two of you. Remember?" Mackenzie teased.

Chloe interrupted their conversation.

"Excuse me, Mackenzie. The men at the front counter are ready to check out, and I need help with using the cash register," she said.

"I'll be right there, sweetie. Chloe, meet my friend Clara. You might as well get used to seeing this pretty face around. She's my best friend and she works over at the Lighthouse company across the street."

"Hi, Chloe, it's nice to meet you." Clara extended her hand.

"Likewise, ma'am."

"Mackenzie, Chloe, I'm going to let you two get back to work. I need to run. I have a fur baby that's waiting for her momma to come home," Clara said.

"All right, but I want you to call me tomorrow and let me know how everything went."

"Will do," Clara said.

She waved to Josh on her way out and caught a few smiles from some of the guys sitting at a nearby table. She had just enough time to make it to the car before the skies let loose and the crackling sound of thunder pierced the sky.

"So much for nice weather," Clara said to herself as she drove home to be with Holly.

~

Clara laid on top of her bed clicking the remote through a rotation of channels she watched regularly. With Holly nestled nearby, it was the perfect evening to drift off to sleep early. First, she'd indulge in a few episodes of Love It or List It. Afterward, she'd listen to an audio book before turning in for the night.

She glanced at the picture on her nightstand beside her bed. It was a picture of her parents, along with herself and her sister, Agnes.

Clara reached over and rubbed her finger across Agnes' face. "Aggy, where did we go wrong? We were supposed to remain close after mom and dad left us," she said.

In the midst of reminiscing, the cell phone startled Clara and sent Holly into a barking frenzy.

"Holly, shh. Settle down, girl. It's okay." She managed to catch Holly and quiet her down in time to pick up the phone.

"Hello?" Clara said. She didn't think to check the number, which she immediately regretted at the sound of the voice on the other end of the line.

"Is this Clara Covington?" he said in a raspy voice.

"Who is this?"

"If you step one foot into the lawyer's building tomorrow, I'll see to it that you never see the light of day again." The call was immediately disconnected.

The words *call ended* flashed on the screen of her cell phone. After moments of standing frozen in disbelief, she frantically mashed a button to reveal the number of the last incoming call.

"Restricted? Dammit," Clara said.

A sense of paranoia started settling in. Was she being watched? Who was the man on the other end of the line, and how did he get her number? Clara's mind flooded with thoughts, yet she was terrified to move from the place where she was standing.

The phone rang again, this time startling her even more than the first time. The caller ID revealed that it was *Lighthouse Tours*.

"Hello?" she answered in a timid voice.

"Hey, Clara, it's Mike. I'm so sorry to bother you. Do you have a minute?"

Clara made an attempt to speak but was rattled to her core. Instead of speaking, she exhaled and then began sobbing on the phone.

"My God. Are you okay?" he asked.

She was choked up and whimpering like an upset child.

"Is somebody there with you?" Mike said.

"No."

"Okay. I need you to breathe. Try to pull it together so you can speak to me. You're making me nervous."

"I... can't...somebody... threatened..." She tried but couldn't stop hyperventilating.

"Are you safe? Do you need me to call the police?" Mike asked.

"I'm fine."

"You are not fine. If you don't tell me what's going on, I can't help you." He tried to reason with her, but she continued to cry.

"I'm heading over to your place. What's your address?" he asked.

"I'm... fine." Clara was being stubborn, but Mike wasn't backing down.

"You're shaken up and you won't let me call the police. If you think for one minute I'm about to get off this phone and leave you like this, think again. Now, give me your address, or I'll look it up in our files if I have to."

"Okay, okay. Are you familiar with the condos by the Putuxant off Solomons Island Road?" she asked.

"Yeah."

She continued taking short little breathes to calm herself down.

"I'm in 2b. The second building, on the top floor. When you arrive at the front gate, I'll buzz you in."

"Okay, I'll be there in ten or fifteen minutes, tops. Keep your doors locked until I get there," he warned.

"Okay," Clara agreed and hung up the phone.

~

"You really didn't have to come over here. I'm sure it was just a prank of some sort."

Mike took a seat next to Clara on the couch. It seemed silly, but she thought she caught a whiff of the Putuxent coming from his clothing. It was probably a result of being out on the boat all afternoon. All of her fears were slowly subsiding and slowly turning into embarrassment instead.

"We haven't known each other that long and I'm already causing drama. This is so embarrassing. I hope you don't think poorly of me. My life is usually pretty boring," she said.

"You have absolutely nothing to be embarrassed about. You were pretty shaken up when I called. What happened?" he asked.

"I got a phone call from a restricted number. A man with a raspy voice told me if I step foot into the lawyer's office tomorrow, he'll see to it that I never see the light of day again. That was it. He hung up after that."

"Did you recognize the voice?" Mike asked.

"No, but I'm almost certain it's somebody from Joan's family. Her niece Olivia called me earlier this week warning me not to try and take anything that belongs to the family. I swear she is absolutely out of her mind. She doesn't know the half. It feels like I've been thrown into a den of lions. I didn't ask to be put in Joan's will. I don't even know what the will says for God's sake. Clearly, they know more than I do. Why else would they view me as such a threat?" The more Clara thought about it, the more angry she became.

"Clara, you have to go to the police. You have to file a complaint," Mike said.

"I wonder whether that will draw even more negative attention my way."

"Leave that up to the police to handle. What they're doing is not okay, and they need to be held accountable," Mike said.

"It's not right, but I think I know a way to resolve this once and for all. I'm not going to the lawyer's office in the morning. It's not worth it."

She wiped the tears from her eyes as she spoke.

"What?" Mike asked.

"I'm serious. I'm not going tomorrow. I'm going to call Joan's lawyer and tell him I want out. I don't want to have anything to do with it. This just proves you can have all the material possessions in the world, and it still won't buy you happiness. Her niece is a prime example. She has everything. Yet, she's still a greedy snake and a creep. I don't want to have anything to do with this anymore." Clara slammed the tissue box down on the coffee table.

"Look, I don't know all the details, but I wouldn't make any rash decisions if I were you," Mike responded.

"I don't think this is a rash decision. If all I have is Joan's memory, then that's more than enough for me. That's all I've ever had all my life. Memories of loved ones to cherish. That's it."

Mike turned and grabbed Clara by the arms. She didn't feel intimidated or frightened. The only thing she felt was safe and cared for.

"Listen to me," he whispered. "There's a right way to go about this and hiding is not the answer. No matter how afraid you may be," Mike said.

"But..." she said.

"Shh, no buts. You can feel safe now. I'm here. I'll go down to the police station with you. And, if you haven't figured it out by now, in situations like these, I'm not taking no for an answer." Mike smiled.

Clara broke her silence with a little laughter and a whole lot of concern for what he must be thinking about her. Go figure. She spent the last ten years of her life relying on the

Young and the Restless for entertainment, and now she was the one at the center of the drama.

"Mike, you must think..."

"Shh," he said as he retreated his hands back to his lap.

"I'll tell you what I think. I think you're a good woman who gave up everything to be there for a dear friend. I also think you're very deserving of whatever it is she's left behind for you. Finally, I think if anyone tries to stand in the way of that... especially by threatening you, then they deserve to deal with the law to the fullest extent," Mike said.

"Oh, and one more thing. From everything that Mackenzie's told me about you, and just in the short period of time I've gotten to know you, I think you're a pretty amazing woman," Mike said.

He got up from the couch and placed his hands in his pockets.

"Now, we have to make a trip to the police station. So, why don't you grab your things, and I'll be right here when you're ready to go," he said.

Clara was stunned and grateful at the same time. She had never met a man who extended such grace and such kindness.

"Thank you," she whispered.

She walked away to grab her things, feeling thankful that she didn't have to go down to the station alone.

CHAPTER 13

On the car ride home from the police station, Clara stared out of Mike's passenger side window with the feeling of fear settling in. Never in her life had she been put in a position where she had to watch over her shoulder and be afraid that somebody wanted to do something harmful to her.

"What are you thinking about?" he asked.

"This whole thing. I went to the police station and filed a report tonight, but now what? It's not like I was able to give them a telephone number. This thing may linger for a while. This morning I left my place peacefully not having to worry about watching over my shoulder. Now, I'm questioning everything," Clara said.

"I already thought about that. I'm willing to camp out on your couch tonight if that will make you feel comfortable. I truly don't believe anybody is following you, but if they are and they see a guy with you, I'm sure they'll be inclined to leave you alone. Besides, whoever called you is a coward. If they really wanted to do something harmful, they would've showed up at your door," he said.

"Mike, I couldn't ask you to do that. You've already done enough. I'm just going to barricade myself in the apartment, and tomorrow I'll leave with a neighbor and head straight to work."

"What about Joan's will?" he asked.

"What about it? I'm serious when I say I want absolutely nothing to do with it. If their mission was to scare me away from claiming whatever she left for me, then mission accomplished," she said.

"I get it. I just think it's kind of sad, that's all. I would at least give the lawyer a call if I were you. I'm almost certain the detective is going to question Olivia. The same way you told the police, maybe it wouldn't hurt for the lawyer to know that she threatened you just a day before you received this mysterious phone call."

Clara didn't respond. She just kept staring out the window trying to figure out a logical plan for moving forward and avoiding this mess at all cost.

"Perhaps Mack can come and hang out with you tomorrow night for a while. Maybe we can set up a little rotating schedule until this whole thing dies down," he said.

"She has Stephanie to think about. The last thing I want to do is be a burden to everyone," Clara said.

"Clara, trust me, you're not being a burden to anyone. You obviously haven't learned much about Solomons Island in the time that you've been out here. I've been here less time than you, and the one thing I know to be true is if you call on your neighbor, they will be there for you. It's what we do. We look out for one another. Now, if you're going to retreat and try and do everything on your own, how can anybody be there for you?" Mike said.

"I guess you're right," Clara replied.

"I know I'm right. It's what being a community is all about.

Now, if there's someone else you'd be more comfortable calling to come stay with you tonight, then I'll leave when they arrive. You can do what you want, but I know you're afraid and you shouldn't be alone," Mike said.

"I don't have anyone to call," she said still looking out the window.

"Well, then, I guess I'm your guy."

Mike turned on the grounds where Clara lived and pulled into a space right next to her car. He asked her to wait inside the car while he checked their surroundings. She even noticed him looking under her car in the side view mirror. Once he was finished, he opened her door and waited for her to exit the car.

"Did you just check under my car?" she asked.

He laughed. "Blame it on Hollywood, okay? You can never be too certain," Mike said.

"Great, thanks for planting that idea in my head. Now, I'm probably going to be checking closets and behind closed doors," she said.

"You'll be fine. I was just doing the guy thing, you know, being protective. Isn't that how it works in the movies? The guy swoops in like a superhero and saves the day." He tried to make Clara laugh.

"That sounds more like a rendition of Superman, don't you think?" She cracked up at the comparison.

Mike rubbed his clean-shaven chin.

"Well, I've always been told I resemble Clark Kent," he said.

Clara lost it and burst into uncontrollable laughter.

"Hey, wait a minute. I'm glad you think it's funny, but I'm serious. Come on, take a closer look at this angle," he said.

"I hate to burst your bubble, but you look absolutely nothing like Clark Kent. Nice try, though," Clara said.

They entered the door of her apartment and properly

secured it for the night. Holly barked at Mike a couple of times but resolved to accepting him once he gave her a little attention.

"Well, I keep telling myself it isn't weird that my boss is spending the night at my place. Hopefully you've convinced yourself of the same?" Clara asked.

"The thought hadn't crossed my mind. Besides, right now, I'm here as your friend and, of course, I mean that in the most respectful way," he said.

"I appreciate it. Can I get you something to drink or something to eat?" she asked.

"I'll take a glass of water. I grabbed a pizza pie after my last tour so I'm good."

"Mike, that reminds me. Did you need something earlier? I never had a chance to find out why you were calling."

Mike snapped his fingers.

"That's right, I almost forgot. I was wondering if you came across any receipts from Jim's Hardware when you were sorting through everything the other day. Brody seems to think there should be a few included in the stack. I thought I'd check with you first before I go tearing up the place to look for them," Mike said.

"No, I don't recall seeing them, but I also don't recommend you tearing up the place. Let's devise an organized plan and tackle this first thing in the morning."

"So, you really plan on skipping out on your appointment with the lawyer tomorrow?" Mike asked.

"Yep. I won't have anything to do with it. It's not worth it," Clara said.

"What do you think Joan would say?" he asked.

"I think she'd be appalled. She's probably rolling over in her grave at the thought of them behaving like this."

"Hmm," Mike said.

Clara prepared a glass of water and laid it on the coffee

table for Mike. She also brought him a pillow and a blanket from her room.

"You're more than welcome to use the shower when you're ready. I have a spare toothbrush and plenty of towels and wash cloths in the linen closet. Just make yourself at home and pick out whatever you'd like," Clara offered.

"Thank you. I'm going to help myself to the remote control and catch up on a little sports news before I get some shut eye. Hopefully, that's all right with you?" Mike said.

"Go right ahead. Help yourself to anything you need."

Clara motioned toward her bedroom door.

"I'm heading to bed. If I don't hit the sack by eleven, I'm useless early in the morning," she said.

"Hey, before you go, I want you to rest easy tonight. If anybody calls your phone again, let me answer it, okay?" Mike tried to reassure Clara.

"Yes, I will. Thanks, Mike."

"Goodnight."

❧

On Friday morning, Ms. Mae approached Jonathan's boat and watched him as he prepared his fishing equipment for the day. He didn't hear her approaching and since she was a little nervous, she waited a few minutes. When he didn't notice her, she reached beyond her comfort zone to get his attention.

"The truth is... I want to make love to you, too, Jonathan."

He dropped his box of fishing hooks and looked up at Mae.

"You see, you were never the issue. I've always cared about you. I even imagined what it would be like to be together... as a couple. But imagining and actually doing... well, that's where I've struggled, until now," she said.

"Anna Mae, if you are trying to get my undivided attention,

130

you have it now more than ever. Did you just say you want to make love to me?" Jonathan cracked a smile.

"Oh, you would focus on that part, wouldn't you?" Mae dismissively waved her hand.

"Heck, yeah. Any man with blood running through his veins would pay attention to that part," Jonathan teased.

He walked over to Ms. Mae and held her hands.

"Mae, we can take our time with this. The idea of us being an item is new, I get it. More than anything, I just want you to know that I love you, Anna Mae. I love you with all my heart," Jonathan confessed.

Tears welled up in Ms. Mae's eyes.

"Why are you crying? This is supposed to be a happy moment," he said.

"I'm just sad that I took so long to open up my heart to you, Jonathan. I'm surprised you put up with me for this long. You really helped me to see things clearly the other day. You were right about every word of it," she confessed.

"I'm not exactly innocent in all this. I could've said something long before now. What's most important is where we go from here." Jonathan placed his lips gently on Ms. Mae's. The adrenaline rush awakened her in ways she hadn't felt in a long time. She could've remained in his embrace for a while if it weren't for the interruption of someone clearing their throat.

"Eh em," Brody said.

"Forgive me, I didn't mean to stop you two love birds. The boss asked me to take a look at your boat before you head out this afternoon, Jonathan." It was obvious that Brody was trying to control the grin on his face, but it wasn't working. Ms. Mae could see right through his little act.

"Wipe that grin off your face, Brody. You act like you never seen grown folks kissing before. I'm getting back to work. Jonathan, I'll see you at my house. Seven o'clock sharp, don't be late," she said. Ms. Mae turned about face and headed back to the office without saying another word. She was partially embarrassed at being busted and partially annoyed that Brody interrupted such a good kiss.

~

Around noon Clara had two missed messages from Joan's lawyer, Dale. Both times he pleaded for her to return his call and expressed disappointment that she hadn't made it to their nine o'clock appointment. By the third call, during Clara's lunch break, she picked up to speak to Dale.

"My goodness, Clara, I've been trying to reach you all morning. Did you forget about our appointment?" he asked.

"No, Dale. I owe you an apology for not calling sooner, but I've made a decision not to participate in all of this. I won't be accepting whatever Joan left for me. You can hand it over to Olivia, whatever it is," she said.

"Excuse me? That's not how this works," he said.

"I know it sounds crazy, but if you only knew the kind of people they are. It's best that I keep my distance," Clara replied.

"Is there something you're not telling me? It's rare to come across someone who would make such a decision," Dale said.

"I'm telling you everything. I just don't want to get caught up in the midst of their family feud, that's all."

The line was quiet for a moment.

"Eh eh, I'm not buying it. I need you to be straight with me, Clara. I'm Joan's lawyer, but we were long-time friends before I ever stepped into the role of becoming her personal lawyer. The one thing I'm certain of was how much she wanted you to be a part of her will. She made an intentional visit to my office to change her will to include you. If you knew all that was involved here, perhaps you wouldn't be so hasty to try and throw it all away. Now, talk to me. What's really going on?"

Clara closed her eyes and recalled the last visit Joan made to his office. She wondered if that was the same day the changes were made. Dale snapped her out of her daydreaming spell.

"Clara, are you still there?"

"Yes, I'm still here. I can't get into it, Dale. I just think it's in my best interest to not get involved," she said anxiously.

"Did Olivia say something to you?" he asked.

The line fell silent again.

"I'll take that as a yes," he said.

"She may have, but I'm making this decision on my own. I know Joan would understand." She tried to sound convincing.

"That's a bunch of crap and you know it. You're not making this decision on your own. I've been in this business long enough to know fear when I hear it. That greedy witch threatened you, didn't she? Let me guess, it was either her or that snake brother of hers. I swear those two have been riding my back like a monkey ever since they landed and I'm sick of it. It's even worse now that they know they're not getting a dime. Joan didn't leave them one penny, and if you ask me, that was a very good call on her part," he said, sounding aggravated.

"I received a call from Olivia earlier this week. She told me if I tried to take anything away from the family, they would put up a fight. Or something to that affect. Yeah, sure, it made me angry, but I've come to expect that behavior from her. But..." Clara hesitated.

"But, last night a man called my phone and threatened that I'd never see the light of day if I stepped foot inside your office. It was awful, Dale. My boss had to take me to the police to file a report. I was too afraid to stay alone in my apartment last night. This is absurd. I can't live my life like this. Over what? A little bit of money? Joan's boat? Whatever it is, it doesn't matter. It's not worth my life. My well-being shouldn't be compromised over this." Clara was hysterical at this point.

"Clara, I'm so sorry. It shouldn't have come to this. I promise to do everything in my power to put this to rest once and for all. Please give me the name of the person you filed the report with. I can help make their job a whole lot easier. I can't prove it, but I have a pretty good hunch about who was behind it all. Greed will make people do crazy things. The truth is, you have something that Olivia and her brother want very badly. And, before I allow you to decline your inheritance, I think it's best we have a face-to-face meeting first," Dale said.

Clara didn't respond. She laid her head back on the head rest and flashed back to her ten-year journey with Joan. *Aww, Joan, why did you have to get me involved in this?* she thought to herself.

"Look. I'm not asking you to commit to anything. I can make a personal visit to your home later this afternoon. That way, you can hear me out, and you don't have to step foot inside my office. What do you say? If not for me, please do it for Joan. Think of it as her one last request."

"Okay," Clara barely whispered.

Dale breathed a loud sigh of relief on the other end of the line.

"In the meantime, you can rest easy in knowing that I'm putting in a phone call to the police station immediately. I'm sure by the time the detective is done with them, you won't be receiving any more unwanted phone calls, if you know what I mean," he suggested.

"Thank you, Dale. My boss said I should've given you a phone call right away. He was right," Clara confessed.

"Smart guy. When we hang up, please text me your address and your contact at the police station. Oh, and one last thing.

What time would you like for me to stop by later on today?" Dale asked.

"Five o'clock work for you?"

"It sure does. I'll see you then. Just remember to text the address to me."

"I will. Thank you, Dale."

"No problem."

～

Toward the last hour of the day, Mike approached Clara once the office was clear.

"Hey, how are you holding up today?" he asked.

"Outside of being exhausted from a lack of sleep, I'm all right. I'm sure it would've been much worse if you weren't around. I can't thank you enough," Clara said.

"That's what a gentleman is supposed to do. Any word from the police?" Mike asked.

"No, and I didn't expect there would be. It's not like they had much to go on last night. An incoming call from a restricted number is not a lot to work with. I ended up speaking to the lawyer this afternoon. By the time I told him everything, he was adamant about giving the police station a call. He seems to think he can make a difference with sharing his side of things. Apparently, Joan's niece and her brother have been stirring up trouble with him and he's had it. Guess they went barking up the wrong tree," Clara said.

"Good. They deserve it. If they're the ones responsible for this, they ought to pay."

Mike tapped his fingers on the front counter and fiddled around a bit.

"So, what's the game plan for tonight? Did you call

Mackenzie or figure out a plan so you don't have to be alone?" Mike asked.

"You know, I thought about it. But, Dale is stopping by the apartment to review the will with me at five. I figured after he leaves, I'll just stay in for the evening. Maybe I'll throw in a little Hollywood action and barricade the door just to be on the safe side." She laughed.

"Ah, look whose being all Hollywood now," Mike teased.

"All jokes aside, if you're still uncomfortable, I'm more than happy to check in on you tonight. It may take a while until you get back to feeling one hundred percent comfortable again," he said.

"Mike, you are too kind. But, you've already gone well beyond the call of duty this week. Since we met, we've gone from car accident, to hiring me as your assistant, to spending the night to protect me from bad guys. Enough is enough already. It's time to return back to some sense of normal, here." She chuckled.

"All right. I'm just offering. At least send me a message to let me know you're okay. It will do wonders for my conscious," Mike said.

"I promise, I will."

"Oh, and let's not forget about Saturday," he said.

"Saturday?"

"Yeah, see. How quickly we forget. I'm not about to allow you to barricade yourself in that apartment all weekend. You're still taking the tour this weekend and so is Holly. A deal is a deal."

"How did Holly get in on this?" Clara asked.

"We bonded over ESPN, chips, and root beer. What can I say?"

"Did you give my dog chips and root beer?" she said with furrowed eyebrows.

"I'm not an idiot. I helped myself to the drink and snacks while Holly hung out with me. She's a sweet dog. Bring her along. I'm sure she'd appreciate the exercise." He cracked a smile.

"I don't know how I allowed you and Mack to talk me into this, but I guess I have to keep my word," Clara agreed.

"Great, I'll pick you guys up. Meet me downstairs at nine."

"I can meet you there," she said.

"No way, then it wouldn't be a surprise. I'll ring your phone when I get there so you don't have to wait outside."

"But..." Clara protested.

"No buts, remember? We're past that. Now, let's shake on it and be done with it. A deal is a deal," he argued.

"Okay."

In the midst of them shaking hands, Savannah peeked her head inside the front door.

"Mike, in case you hadn't noticed, I've been sitting out here in the car for the past fifteen minutes. You think you can stop talking to red long enough to join me?" she asked sarcastically.

Clara assumed that red was her new nickname. It was funny how Savannah managed to talk about Clara and even talk down to her without ever establishing a real reason for it.

Mike rolled his eyes and turned to address Savannah.

"I'll be right there. We were just wrapping up," he said with very little enthusiasm.

The whole thing made Clara wonder why he would ever entertain spending time with someone like that.

CHAPTER 14

Clara dialed the appropriate numbers on her phone to release the front gate and let Dale into the parking lot. By the time she finished drying her last set of dishes there was a rapid tapping sound at the front door. On the other side of the peep hole Dale stood in a pinstriped suit with a briefcase in hand. She flung her dish towel over her shoulder, took a deep breath, and unlocked the door to let him in.

"Dale, how are you? Please come on in," she said.

"I'm well, thank you."

"That's good. Did you have any trouble finding your way here?" she asked.

"No, not at all. Your directions were rather easy to follow. I can't believe in all the years I've been living here that I've never been to this place," he said.

"I could say the same up until this year. You're not alone."

Holly growled at Dale, which was an improvement from her usual barking.

"Oh, Holly, it's okay. Mind your manners, sweet girl." She tried to console Holly.

"Dale, I should've given you the heads up about Holly. She's real sweet once she warms up to you. Hopefully, you're not allergic to pets, are you?" Clara asked.

"Not at all. Hey, this is her house, not mine. She's just protecting her territory, that's all."

"Thanks for being understanding. Please, have a seat on the couch. Can I offer you something to drink?" she asked.

"I'm fine, thank you. I'm just going to loosen up my tie a bit and get right down to business with you. The wife and kids are planning a special anniversary meal for me tonight, and I promised them I would be home on time." Dale smiled.

"Oh, well, happy anniversary to you."

"Thank you. You know you've been married a pretty long time when anniversaries start to become a family affair." He laughed.

"I'll bet."

"All right. Down to the reason for my visit. First thing I want to share is I talked to the detective you filed the report with. We had quite a lengthy discussion, and it looks like he has his work cut out for him. Olivia and her family have already flown back home. She lives in Texas and the brother in South Carolina. I don't know that he'll get too far with this, but he did mention something about pulling their phone records, so we'll have to wait and see where that goes. In the meantime, I'm almost certain your troubles left the minute they boarded those planes, so hopefully that helps to put your mind at ease," he said.

"Thank you for that."

"No problem. I shared with him that Olivia had a lot of reason to be angry with you. She came across a copy of Joan's will at the house prior to our meeting on Friday. As a result, she knew what to expect from our meeting on Friday and wasn't too pleased about it," Dale explained.

"Well, what did the will say that would leave Olivia so bent out of shape?"

Dale slid the document closer to where Clara could see and began highlighting the important parts line by line.

"I, Joan C. Russell, hereby declare my executor, Dale Davidson of Davidson and Associates, to distribute my assets as follows," Clara read aloud.

Dale picked up where Clara left off.

"If you follow the remainder of this section, you'll see that Joan left you all of the funds remaining in her bank accounts, her stocks, bonds, and retirement funds. She also left you the beach house here in Solomons, her car, and she wanted you to have Holly. Her accounts alone add up to the sum of two and a half million dollars. That's not even including the value of the house."

The lining of Clara's stomach began to feel queasy. It was a different kind of feeling from being in the boat, nevertheless very unsettling. She began salivating but pulled it together in time to respond to Dale who was repeatedly calling her name.

"Clara, are you all right? You look pale."

"Uh, no," she said.

"No, you're not all right?"

"No, as in, hell no, I'm not accepting this. Joan made a mistake."

"I don't understand. She didn't make a mistake. Everything is spelled out here as plain as day. Joan even included a no contest clause so that no one could challenge the validity of the will," Dale said.

"You don't understand. This is the reason why Olivia was trying to get me to sign legal documents and threatening me. No way am I getting caught up in the middle of this. I don't know anything about maintaining a fancy house and a big bank account. But more importantly, that woman will try to hunt me down for the rest of my life if I accept this. I can't. I won't do it."

"There's no threat or legal document that Olivia could ever ask you to sign that will change Joan's wishes. And, you're not caught up in the middle of anything. The house and all the funds, the car, the boat, it's all in your name. I'll put it to you this way. I don't know what you did exactly, but you damn sure left an impression on that woman's heart. A year ago today, she marched right into my office and made one of the biggest decisions of her life by adding you to her will. You need to take that into consideration before you toss away everything she and her husband worked so hard for," Dale said.

Clara massaged her temples. She didn't know whether to be mad, or what to feel. Dale's message tugged on her heart, but she also had no desire to compete with Olivia's greed. To this day, greed was also the root of division between Clara and her sister, Agnes.

"There's one last thing," he said.

Dale laid an envelope on the table with Joan's handwriting on the front. The letter was addressed to Clara.

"It's a letter from Joan. I want you to do me a favor. Wait 'til I'm gone. Pour yourself a glass of wine and read it. Take the weekend to think things over, and get back to me next week with your decision."

Dale gathered his belongings and stood up to leave.

"Dale," Clara said.

"Yes?"

"I was just wondering. Did Joan leave anything to Olivia and her brother?" she asked.

"Yes, as a matter of fact, she did. We'll never know what's inside, but they received an envelope with their names addressed on the front as well," he responded.

"I see," she said, while rising up to see him to the front door.

Dale paused before exiting her apartment.

"I look forward to hearing from you next week." He extended his hand to shake Clara's.

After he left, she secured the door and gently slid to the floor to hang her head in utter disbelief.

∽

Later that evening Clara called Mack. "Good Lord, Clara! You're a millionaire? Seriously? This is the kind of crap you usually hear about on television. What in the world are you going to do with all that money?" Mackenzie asked.

"I haven't accepted the money," she said.

"But, you're going to, right? You'd have to be delusional not to."

"Not everything is about money, Mack. I told you, the last time I had this debate was with my sister, Agnes, and it didn't end well. It was one of the last times we spoke, remember?" Clara said.

"Ahh, so that's what this is all about. You're over there comparing apples to oranges. What happened between you and your sister has nothing to do with this and you know it."

"Do I?" Clara asked.

"By now, you should know that you can't control the behavior of others. You chose to do your job with honor, you chose to be there for Joan as a friend, and to care for her. In return, she chose to leave you in her will. It's a blessing, not a curse. Stop treating it as such," Mackenzie said in a stern voice.

"Now, I'm with Dale. Pour yourself that glass of wine and open up the letter and read it. Don't make me have to come over there and knock some sense into you, Clara," Mackenzie warned.

Clara cracked a smile and fought back a few tears.

"You still don't even know the half. I didn't get a chance to tell you about the threat I received earlier in the week. I think Olivia was behind it for sure. Somebody called and threatened that I wouldn't see the light of day if I stepped foot inside the lawyer's office on Friday. He had to come to my place today just to help put my mind at ease," she said.

"What?" Mack sounded shocked.

"Yes, can you believe that? Mike went down to the station with me to file a report. If he hadn't called that night, I don't know what I would've done. He even stayed the night just to be certain I was safe," Clara said.

"Wait a minute. This is insane. When did all of this happen?"

"Yesterday. Trust me, this week has been a whirlwind. I'm ready to go back to the boring and mundane lifestyle that I once lived. I miss the simple things like taking long walks on the beach to feel rejuvenated. Or getting excited about visiting the café toward the end of the week. I didn't sign up for all this drama. And for what, a house and a few possessions that can easily be replaced? No thank you!" Clara declared.

"Clara, at the end of the day, do you really think they would go as far as trying to harm you?"

She laid flat on her bed glancing at the popcorn ceiling in her apartment.

"Probably not. I know they're just empty threats, but still..."

"Well, I'm glad you know it, because from what I could tell, Olivia is nothing but a coward. And, by the way, those long walks that you miss so much. You can start taking them again, you know. You do own the place."

The line fell silent for a moment.

"And, what's this about Mike staying with you? How convenient for your knight in shining armor to come to the rescue. I knew there was a sparkle in his eye the night he brought you to the café," Mackenzie said.

"It's no big deal. I was afraid and he offered to stay over. Listen, I have to run and get Stephanie's dinner together, but I want you to call me if you need anything. I also want to hear an update on what you decided. It's just my two cents, but I wouldn't make this decision without giving it a lot of thought," Mackenzie said.

"Thanks, Mack"

"All right love, talk to you later."

~

After her last sip of Chardonnay, Clara carefully opened the envelope and removed a handwritten letter. She recognized Joan's familiar cursive handwriting and immediately held her breath. The letter was dated one year prior.

"Clara, by the time you read this I imagine I'll be partying with the angels. There's no way that I'm going to let cancer have the last word. I'm going to go peacefully and with joy knowing that I was able to live a good life and spend my last days with a friend like you. You showed up at my doorstep at a time when I needed so much more than a housekeeper. I was a lonely widow in need of a friend. You never cared about my possessions, and you never tried to take advantage. You just loved me. And, for that, I am forever grateful. Now, it's my turn to show my appreciation. I can't think of a person who is more deserving. I hope that you will accept my home and fill it with all the love and joy that it once had when my Paul was alive. I'm also leaving you with the necessary means to keep the place up and running. The only thing I ask of you is to please take care of my sweet Holly. She's a loyal pal, and I know how much she adores you. Finally, take care of yourself. Laugh, forgive, and smile as much as you can. Live life without regrets. Most important of all, open your heart up to love again. Take care. Until we meet again, Love Joan."

Clara's breathing simmered down to its normal pattern. She felt a great sense of sadness and relief, similar to how she felt when she lost her parents. She beckoned for Holly to come join her at the bottom of the bed and then laid in the fetal position until she finally fell asleep.

CHAPTER 15

*O*n Saturday morning, Mike pulled up to the front of Clara's building and beeped his horn. She spotted him from across the quad and tugged at Holly's leash. With the top of the Jeep removed and the sun beaming on his face, he looked like he was ready for adventure. He had an effortless, rugged, yet handsome appeal about him that she was trying hard to ignore.

"Did you get my text about bringing a pair of sandals just in case?" he asked.

"Yep, I did." Clara placed Holly in the back with her backpack and then hopped in the front next to Mike.

"New car?" she asked.

"Not really. I just take it out on the weekends or whenever I'm not working," he said.

"Nice, I like it. It suits you."

"Thank you." Mike smiled.

"Should I be nervous about this tour? I have no idea where we're going."

"Absolutely not. You and Holly are in good hands. If it

makes you feel better to know, we're going to Calvert Cliffs. Typically, we'd head up to the Chesapeake, but I promised to keep you on dry land, so here we are," Mike said.

Clara fastened her seatbelt and slipped on her sunglasses. Her hair was whipping in the wind, but she didn't care. She embraced the carefree feeling that it gave her.

"Do you normally leave the Island when you're giving tours?" she asked.

"Of course, all the time. There's so much to see from here all the way up the Chesapeake Bay. Why would I limit the tours?"

"Guess you have a good point. The more places you go the better it is for business, right?" she said.

"Exactly. But, today we're going to travel a few miles up route four, and we'll be there in no time. You ready for an adventure, Holly girl?" Mike yelled to the back.

Clara checked the back to see happy Holly wagging her tail.

"This is so good for her. We haven't been able to get out much since we moved."

Mike pointed to Clara.

"According to Mackenzie, you haven't been able to get out much at all. But, we're going to fix that."

"Oh gosh," she said.

"No, oh gosh. It's time to get out and live," Mike said.

"You sound just like Joan."

"I'll bet she was a very wise woman." He paused for a moment and then said, "So, how did things work out yesterday with you and the lawyer? Did you get everything straightened out?"

Clara sighed. She was still grappling with making the right decision.

"Uh, oh, that doesn't sound too good," he said.

"No, it's not that. I just...I don't know what to do, that's all. I have a huge decision before me, and I don't know what to do. It's fine, I'm sure I'll sort it out eventually," Clara said.

"Okay, just tell me the lawyer spoke to the police on your behalf, that's all I want to know."

"Yes, he did. Dale has been great. Apparently, Olivia was hounding him, and he has his own stories to share with the detective. I was able to confirm that she and her brother are back home now. Plus, I haven't received any further calls, so that's always nice," Clara confessed.

"Good. I'm glad to hear it. Promise me you won't be shy about reaching out if you need anything. I'm sure I can speak for myself and Mackenzie when I say that we're here for you."

The way Mike comforted her, the way he looked in her eyes, almost as if he was looking deep into her soul, made her forget about being on an outing with her boss. There was a chemistry between them, and it was only growing more electrifying.

Clara heard the tune to Sweet Caroline playing on the radio. When Mike caught her humming along, he turned the radio up and sang along to the main chorus. With her hair blowing in the wind and her favorite tunes playing, Clara temporarily forgot about everything that was weighing her down.

"Wow, you're carrying a nice set of vocals there. Were you ever part of a chorus of some sort?" Mike asked.

"Not quite, but I was a member of a one-man band called the shower club," she teased.

"Ha ha, even I can sing in the shower. The difference is you sound nice even without the enhanced acoustics."

Just then Mike pulled into a parking space at Calvert Cliffs.

"Here we are. I thought we could hit the red trail and take it all the way out to the beach. Maybe even collect some fossils along the way if you're into that sort of thing." Mike hopped out of the jeep and grabbed his hiking equipment in the back.

"Wait a minute. Are you trying to tell me you bring your boat tours to an outdoor fossil park?" Clara asked.

"Hey, hey, this is more than just an outdoor fossil park. And, no, I don't bring them into the park, but our clients ask us for referrals and places to visit all the time. It always goes over well if you can speak from experience. It sounds a whole lot more genuine."

Clara held her hands up in surrender.

"I get it. You are all about the experience, aren't you?" she asked.

"In my industry, you have to be."

Clara grabbed Holly and followed Mike into the entrance of the park.

~

Mike and Clara were the only two on the beach. They were surrounded by the tranquil sound of miniature waves crashing along the shore and tall cliffs that continued for miles. He pulled out a couple of towels and a brown paper bag lunch for the two of them to enjoy. Holly was content with a dog bone that Clara had given her.

"You seem rather quiet. Is everything okay?" he asked.

"Everything is lovely. I'm sorry, I must've gotten lost in my thoughts for a little while. I know you and Mackenzie tease me about not getting out enough. But, the one thing I used to do religiously was take walks along the beach. It gave me time to think."

"Ah, okay. That's a good thing. I was just hoping I wasn't boring you to death." Mike smiled.

"No way, are you kidding me? You can never go wrong with bringing me to the beach. Don't get me wrong, the park is beautiful and all, but the beach is my happy place," Clara said.

Several minutes passed with silence as they finished eating and taking in the view. A family passed by with boys who were thrilled to find a shark's tooth in the sand. Finally, Clara broke her silence.

"Mike, I have a confession to make."

"What's on your mind?" he responded.

"I... I..." Clara struggled with saying what was on her heart.

"Shh, you don't have to say anything. I feel the same way," he said.

They looked in each other's eyes and leaned closer, and then a little bit closer and kissed each other softly on the lips. Mike paused to see that she was okay with the kiss, but Clara drew closer to experience his lips once more. After indulging each other a while longer, the sound of children approaching caused them to withdraw.

"Oh, no. What have I done?" Clara hung her head in shame.

"Don't be upset. You didn't do anything. Maybe I misunderstood, but I thought..." Mike's words trailed off as he tried to read what Clara was thinking.

"You didn't misunderstand anything, Mike. I gave you an open invitation to kiss me and didn't exactly ask you to stop."

"Yeah, but now I've created this awkward moment for you and that's the last thing I wanted to do. I thought you were trying to tell me that you feel something between us. Either way, I was wrong. I'm supposed to be the professional here. Please forgive me."

"Mike, please. You don't have to explain yourself. We're

both adults here and let's face it, the attraction between us is real. But, that's not what I was going to say earlier," Clara said.

Mike relaxed and positioned himself to listen to Clara.

"I was going to thank you for bringing me here. Walking along the beach got me to thinking about the important decision I have to make. I was reminded that not only is this a place where I have fond memories of Joan, but it's also a place where I find peace, and rest, and a place where I can think, and feel rejuvenated," she said.

"Okay... well, I'm glad I was able to help you make the connection. Now, I feel even worse. I thought you were about to say something completely different." He laughed.

"I told you not to feel bad. I wanted that kiss just as much as you did." She placed her hand over Mike's hand.

"To be honest, I'm grateful for the job, but I kinda thought you were cute the night we met. I had no idea I would see you when I came in the next day to apply. I probably should've left the moment I realized you owned the place." Clara was candid with him. He seemed to be into her just as much as she was into him. But, she couldn't neglect the fact that he was her boss first, and he also had a lady friend in his life.

"But, listen. There's something else that I need to tell you. Something I've been considering, and since you played a major role in helping me out this week, I think you should know," she said.

"Is everything okay?" he asked.

"Yeah, everything is fine. I don't know how to say this, but I guess I'll just come out with it. Joan left me everything in her estate."

"Okay," Mike said.

"I mean, everything. And, should I decide to accept it... well... it would be life changing.

There would be a lot more flexibility in the decisions I

make going forward with my savings, where I choose to live, and things along those lines," Clara explained.

"So you're thinking of leaving? I guess that's a ridiculous question for me to ask. If you have the means to pick up and move wherever you want, why would you need to stay, right?" Mike tried to laugh it off but wasn't doing such a good job at masking his feelings.

"Mike, I just meant that I have more flexibility about where I choose to live in Solomons Island. Whether I keep Joan's home or not. I'm not leaving the island. I love being here. I adore living near the water, I love hanging at the café with Mack, and I love my new job. What would my days be like without organizing receipts or listening to Ms. Mae complain?" She chuckled.

"Yeah, you have a good point there," he agreed.

"I just want to make sure that you still want me there after all that's taken place this week. I crossed the lines of profession-alism in so many ways. I don't even recognize this version of myself. Plus, I know you have Savannah in your life. And, well... I apologize," she said, feeling ashamed.

"Savannah? Please! We're not an item. We used to date a while back, but that's been over for a long time now. That stunt she pulled with kissing me the other day was an act because you were there. She's jealous of you, if you haven't figured it out," he said.

"But, she came back again yesterday to see you. She was waiting out in the car for you and everything," Clara said.

"Yeah, I know. She called me minutes beforehand and begged me to come help her father with unloading a big delivery at the house. She treats me like I'm still her boyfriend every now and again, and I guess I'm guilty of never saying no. But, trust me, there's nothing there, I promise," Mike declared.

"Well, even still. I am your assistant, and we have to be able to conduct ourselves professionally if we're going to work together, don't you think?"

Mike placed one hand gently behind her head and planted another succulent kiss on her lips. Any thoughts of being professional would have to be preserved for Monday morning.

CHAPTER 16

*O*n Monday morning, Mike held his traditional monthly meeting with the staff. Brody, Jonathan, and Ms. Mae gathered around the conference table. Clara pulled out a chair at the opposite end of the table away from Mike.

Okay, just take notes and don't make too much eye contact, Clara thought to herself.

Although Saturday was absolutely perfect with Mike, she didn't want to blow it at work. It was bad enough that Ms. Mae possessed a sixth sense about these things. The last thing Clara wanted to do was give her something to talk about.

"Good morning, everyone. I know we have a couple of tours this morning, so I'm just going to jump right in out of respect for everyone's time. For starters, I'd like to thank you all for a wonderful kick off to our spring tours. A ton of feedback is starting to pour in from our clients and they couldn't be more pleased." Mike thanked everyone individually.

"Now, on to more good news. As a result of the wonderful work that you've been able to provide here at Lighthouse Tours and in preparation for this summer, we'll be adding a new addition to our team. Hopefully within the next month," he said.

Ms. Mae looked at Mike with an expression of concern.

"Now, Ms. Mae, I knew you would give me that look, but don't you worry. As long as your doctor approves, I'll be ramping up your workload back to what you're accustomed to," Mike assured her.

Ms. Mae breathed a sigh of relief and chuckled a little bit.

"You all know how I feel about bringing in new people. We have a pretty good thing going here, and I hesitate to disrupt that in any way. However, the workload is growing by leaps and bounds, and we could use the extra help. Besides, bringing Clara on the team worked out pretty well, and I'm hopeful we'll be just as lucky next time around." Mike looked at Clara and smiled.

She returned the smile to Mike and then to the whole team.

"We love having you here, Clara," Ms. Mae said.

"Thank you, I still have a lot to learn, but I'm really grateful to be here. I think Lighthouse Tours is turning out to be a really good fit for me," she responded.

"Well, that's good news because we need all hands on deck to help tackle the season ahead. We have the remainder of spring and then summer, which is our busiest season of the year. I'm looking to hire another tour guide who can preferably take my place, and I will serve as a fill in for the rest of you, as needed. Eventually, if we keep it up at this pace, we'll look at expanding even further, but I don't want to get too far ahead of myself," he said.

"I think that sounds like a good plan, Mike. Let me know if you need me to pick up an extra shift or two until you find someone," Jonathan said.

"Yeah, boss, that makes two of us. I'm ready to get out there. I was born ready," Ms. Mae said.

"I appreciate that. Oh, and Brody, I almost forgot. You and I may need to go boat shopping soon. The current boats are up to par and the maintenance records look pretty good, but let's sit down later on this week and look over a few options for adding another boat to the fleet."

"Yes, sir. I already have a few options in mind that you might like," he said.

"Fantastic. The only other thing that comes to mind is a few ideas I've been tossing around for our evening tours." Mike turned toward Jonathan and Ms. Mae.

"Jonathan... Ms. Mae... not to put you on the spot or anything, but how would you two like the idea of offering a few couples' tours? You know, something with a romantic date night theme," Mike said with a grin on his face.

"Why us?" Ms. Mae asked.

"Ms. Mae, come on. I can't think of a better couple to ask. I see the fire in your eyes when the two of you look at each other. Let me guess. I bet you thought the rest of us were clueless, didn't you?" Mike teased.

Jonathan smiled really big at the sight of Ms. Mae squirming in her seat and trying to explain her way out of this.

"Mike, you're just as bad as Brody, minding grown folks' business," she said.

"I'm not minding your business at all, Ms. Mae. All I'm saying is, I think you two would make a good fit for the tour. Think about it, and if you're interested, let me know," Mike replied.

Clara let out a little laughter along with Jonathan. It was all fun and games for Ms. Mae unless she was the one in the spotlight.

"I guess it's no secret. We might as well let the cat out the bag. News spreads real fast around here, anyway. All it takes is sitting down for one meal at the café and that's all she wrote.

All of our business will be on the front page of the newspaper by the next morning," she said.

"Well, Ms. Mae, I'm not looking to spread your business. I just know talent when I see it, and I think you two would make a dynamic duo. In more ways than one," Mike said.

Ms. Mae rose up from the table and grabbed her purse.

"I'm all for anything that helps pay the bills and adds value to the business. Jonathan will get back to you with his thoughts," Ms. Mae said.

Everyone rolled their chairs back and gathered their belongings.

"By the way, Mike. You're not the only one who recognizes a dynamic duo when you see one." Ms. Mae winked at Mike and walked out of the room. Clara kept her head down, too mortified to look up and see the response from everyone remaining in the room.

～

That evening at the café, Mackenzie joined Clara in a booth near the window. Ms. Mae and Jonathan were eating at the front counter, and Joshua popped a coin in the juke box to help liven the place up a bit. Chloe was becoming a pro at the cash register and had a knack for multitasking, so the part time gig was working out pretty well for her. The new owner of the café made his appearance to check on the place, but he gave Mack a promotion. So, ultimately, when he wasn't around, she was the boss in charge.

"Mack, I'm proud of you. Not too long ago you were worried about losing your job and look at you now. You run this place!" Clara said.

"Well, thankfully, the new guy took the advice of our former owner, so here I am. He's not so bad. He pops his head in a couple times a month to make sure everything is running smoothly, but he leaves the rest up to us. He made some minor changes, but for the most part, he seems like more of an investor than anything else. I guess things worked out in my favor in the end. Steph and I could sure use the raise," Mack said.

"What about you? Catch me up on everything. I feel like I'm out of the loop." She continued.

"Where do I begin?"

Clara leaned back in her chair.

"I think I've made my decision about Joan's will," Clara said.

"What are you going to do?"

"I'm calling Dale tomorrow to let him know that I'm accepting my inheritance. I was hesitant at first, but this was Joan's wish. Mack, she arranged this last year. I had no idea the last time I drove her to see Dale that she was making arrangements that would forever change my future. She also left a letter expressing to me all the things that I wish I had a chance to say to my parents when they died. She thanked me, Mack. She wished me well. She desires for me to fill her place with all the love and joy she used to share with her husband. Now, I can't make any promises that I'll do any of that to perfection, but I can damn sure try. Why would I let somebody like Olivia scare me out of such an opportunity?" Clara asked.

"Now, we're talking." Mackenzie banged the table with her fists.

The customers in the surrounding area turned around to look.

"Sorry," Mackenzie whispered.

"You know, Mack, it didn't even hit me until Mike took me to the beach on Saturday."

"Excuse me? The beach? Do tell!" Mack said.

"Oh, I will. But, listen. It all came back to me the moment I started feeling those waves crashing against my feet and the sand between my toes. I used to love spending time at the beach behind Joan's house." She leaned closer.

"It was the place where I prayed and talked to my parents. It was my place to think and to find freedom from everything that haunted me in my past. Like my broken relationship with my sister, Agnes. Joan is giving me so much more than just a house and some money. She's giving me a place where I find peace. And, you know, Mack. Somehow deep down inside, I think she knew how much I loved it out there."

"See there. I couldn't be more happy for you, Clara." Mack hugged Clara from across the table. "Now, I love you and all, but this time you're going to hire a moving company to do all the heavy lifting. I'm not lugging that big old mattress back down those stairs again. I can tell you that right now!" Mackenzie laughed.

"I wouldn't dare ask you to."

"Do you think you're going to be able to live in that big house by yourself?" Mackenzie asked.

"I hadn't thought that far in advance, but I'll figure something out. I kind of grew accustomed to the place with Holly there."

"What about your job? And Mike? What is going on with Mike?" Mackenzie was through the roof with excitement.

"I plan on keeping my job. You know I'm just a down to earth regular girl who caught a lucky break. All I know is work. I still need something to keep me busy during the day and that's not going to change," she said.

"As for Mike, on Saturday he gave me my first tour. I could wring your neck for encouraging him to do that, Mack. Don't get me wrong, hiking the red trail out at Calvert Cliffs to the beach was amazing. In a lot of ways, it was just what I needed to help clear my mind. But, I'm ashamed to admit, the day ended with a kiss. With multiple kisses to be exact," Clara confessed.

"I knew it! See, I told you he was a good fit for you."

"Yeah, but Mack, come on. Everything about this is so out of character for me. I feel like I stumbled into a new career that I really like, but making out with the boss? Seriously?" Clara whispered and looked around the café.

"I don't care what you say, Clara. You can't ignore how you feel. It's too late to turn back the clock now. What are you going to say to him? 'Sorry, I should've walked away when I realized I was attracted to you,'" Mackenzie said.

"Actually, I did say that in so many words. But, in the end, I reassured him that I'm grateful for the job and I plan on keeping things very professional when we're at work."

"Key words being... when you are at work. Once you're off the clock he's fair game, girl." Mackenzie twirled a pretend lasso in the air.

"Will you hush. Ms. Mae and Jonathan are sitting right over there. You know that woman knows everything," Clara said.

"She sure does, but right now she's caught up in her own love affair, so she may be too pre-occupied to keep up with your business, if you know what I mean."

"Ha, that's what you think," Clara said.

"So, are the two of you going to see each other again?" Mackenzie asked.

"We didn't make any plans. I'm into him and all, but I don't want to complicate things. Imagine how awkward it would be if things started to go south between us? Then, I would have to leave my job for real."

"So? You can afford to do that now. Here's a piece of sound advice for you. Live your life. That's it. Period," Mackenzie said.

Clara shook her head and smiled at her dear friend. She was thankful for her wit, her sass, and her wisdom. Mack was giving her the kick in the pants that she needed.

"And as for tomorrow, I want you to march right down to Dale's office and claim what's yours. I'll go with you if you want me to," she offered.

"Thanks, Mack. I could use the moral support."

"Consider it done. So, tell me..." Mack looked around before continuing further.

"Is he a good kisser?" she asked.

"Yes," Clara said laughing heartily at the question.

"Mack, you don't understand. I finally pulled it together in the end. But, I didn't want to," she confessed.

"Man! How did you two end up locking lips to begin with?"

"Honestly, I was trying to tell him that going to the beach brought back good memories and was helpful in my decision making. I was struggling to find the right words at first. You know how it is when you're trying to walk that fine line of not being too personal but at the same time wanting to share. He was so helpful to me the other night and all, I just thought I would let him know what was going on. But, I think he misunderstood and thought I was trying to reveal my feelings for him. Anyway, one thing led to another and next thing I know, he kissed me," Clara said.

"Girl, you know you're hot stuff when you land yourself a job, a beachfront inheritance, and a man, all in the same week!"

"Oh, Mack, you need to quit while you're ahead!" Clara chuckled. "It didn't exactly happen in a week and for the record, I don't have a man," she said.

"Mmm hmm, it's just a matter of time. You two are so hot for each other we're not going to be able to pry you apart. You just wait and see. I'm happy for you. It's about time things start looking upward. I think Joan would be proud of you, too. You made the right choice, Clara," Mack said.

"I sure hope so. You and Stephanie might have to pack your things and come live with me."

"No, ma'am. I'm sure it will only be a matter of time before you'll be needing your privacy. You know, there are plenty of people out there who meet on the job and fall in love. And, there are plenty of couples who run businesses together. I'm just saying."

"Okay, now you're getting too far ahead. For right now, I'm the assistant, that's it. Agreed?" Clara asked.

"I'm not agreeing to anything. If you want to believe that, it's on you. Now, are you having your usual today, or are you going to pick out a celebratory meal and beverage to enjoy this evening?"

"I'll have my usual plus tonight's special. And, since we're celebrating, why not bring out a glass of your finest wine. I need something to help me unwind a little," Clara said.

"That's the spirit. One house special, a glass of fine wine, and your usual cheesecake, coming right up," Mack said.

As Mackenzie left the table, Clara noticed a mature group of couples enjoying a round of gin rummy. It caused her to daydream of growing old and experiencing the simple pleas-antries of life. She hoped one day she had someone to sit in the café with and tease over a card game. But, most important of all, she vowed to stay true to herself, to appreciate the simple things, and not let her newfound inheritance change who her parents raised her to be.

CHAPTER 17

With each soft kiss on the back of her neck, Ms. Mae felt herself falling deeper into the abyss of Jonathan's love. He was gentle with her, he was kind, and he was everything that she now wanted and needed in a mate. *How did I overlook his tenderness and affection for me?* she quietly thought to herself. But, her thoughts were interrupted with his sweet distractions.

"Jonathan, if I don't stop you now, I'm not going to be able to think straight," she said.

"That's the whole point, dear. You're not supposed to think about it. Just relax and let all the stress of the day melt away."

"No, no. We'll have plenty of time for that, but tonight I want to talk to you about something that's been on my mind," Ms. Mae said.

"Why, sure. Is everything okay?"

"Yes, everything is fine. I just feel like I want to make up for lost time," she said.

"What do you mean, Mae? I thought we've been doing a pretty good job of that these last few nights. Don't you agree?"

"I don't mean in a physical sense, Jonathan. I'm talking about being open with the family about us being together now. My folks have only known you as my friend. Don't you think if we're going to be together, it should be more official with those that we love?" Ms. Mae asked.

Jonathan grazed his hand across Ms. Mae's cheek.

"Are you the same woman I've known all these years? I can't believe what I'm hearing right now." He kissed her at the center of her forehead.

"Mae, you won't get any arguments out of me. I prayed for the day that your heart would be open to me in this way. It would bring me great joy to share this with the family. I'll tell your daughter, your sister, my folks, heck I'll tell the whole world if you want me to," Jonathan said.

Ms. Mae let out a sigh. She realized she was the only one that needed to arrive at these kinds of decisions. Jonathan's heart was in it wholeheartedly and had been there for quite some time.

"I don't know how you managed all these years to wait so patiently for me to come around," she said.

"It was worth the wait, Mae. You're my best friend. I wouldn't have it any other way."

"But, what if I'd said no? What if I rejected the idea of us being together? That would've ruined everything, including our friendship," she said.

Jonathan took Ms. Mae by the hand to lead her to the window seat in her bedroom.

"Mae, this might sound crazy to you, but I've always known in my heart that you would be a part of my life one way or the other. Don't get me wrong, there was only one way that made the most logical sense to me, but if I couldn't have you, I was willing to be your friend. I mean, think about it. I've been around long enough to watch your daughter Lily grow into a fine young woman and have children of her own. Then there's your sister. I've been around long enough to watch her get divorced and remarry again," he said.

Ms. Mae got a good chuckle out of the whole thing. It was true. Jonathan could probably talk about the family and tell stories just as good as any of them could. Now that she thought of it, the family would probably wonder why it took her so long to come around. Her sister used to prod her several years ago about getting out there and meeting someone. It was as if they all knew there would come a time when Mae would desire love again.

"Hopefully, this conversation has helped to put your mind at ease. I'm in it for the long haul, Mae. You can count on that," Jonathan said.

"You sure you won't get sick of me? I mean, by the time we start doing tours together, and then spending time outside of work together, you may change your mind."

"I could say the same about you, Mae. But, I won't because I trust what's happening on the inside of your heart. I'm going to ask you to do the same." He placed Ms. Mae's hands over his heart.

Ms. Mae could feel Jonathan's heart beating with anticipation. She slowly drew near and delivered a sweet kiss and caressed him. The two became entangled to the extent that talking was no longer an option.

~

On Tuesday morning, Clara sat on the opposite side of Dale's desk waiting to sign important paperwork. His secretary delivered her file and placed a hot cup of coffee on the desk beside Clara.

"Thank you, Marie," she said.

"No problem. Let me know if you need anything else," Dale's secretary said while exiting the room.

"Well, Dale, I have some good news to share with you," Clara said.

"The mere fact that you're here and accepting what is rightfully yours is good news. I can't imagine what else you might have to share."

"I received a call from detective Monahan yesterday afternoon. Turns out he was able to do a little digging and pulled Olivia's phone records and her brother's phone records," she said.

"Ooh, did he find anything good?" Dale asked.

"Olivia's record came up squeaky clean. Her brother's cell phone record was not as clean. Monahan said there was an outgoing call to my number, at the precise date and time I received the threatening phone call."

"Get out. You mean to tell me the moron didn't have enough sense to at least use a different phone? He had to be desperate. Or maybe he assumed you would be so scared out of your mind that you wouldn't do anything about it," Dale said.

"I was scared out of my mind. My boss had to spend the night with me and for God's sake, you had to come to my place because I was too afraid to set foot inside your office. If I hadn't received a call from the detective, I still might not be here today."

"I don't blame you. So, what are you going to do about it? Are you going to press charges?" Dale asked.

"I should, but I don't know. Somehow, I don't feel nearly as frightened now that I know who was behind it all. I had my suspicions, but I always suspected one of them put somebody up to doing their dirty work. Monahan said he scared the daylights out of the brother when he called to ask a few questions. Honestly, I feel like my biggest revenge is being here today, signing these papers, and walking off with the very thing they tried to scare me away from," Clara said.

"Better you than me. I'd still have to teach them one last lesson to make sure they never mess with me again. I'd think about that one if I were you."

"I will," she said.

"As for today, you are here for good reasons, so let's not spoil all the fun. In this envelope I'm holding, you'll find what I call the keys to the kingdom. Every key you can possibly imagine is in here. I even had Marie stop by the place and label each set so you'll know what's what. The only thing I want to caution you about is the staging furniture that yours truly ordered before she left. Olivia was so certain the house was hers that she was having it staged for a realtor. What an idiot," he said.

"She did mention something about a realtor, but by then I was too consumed with what I was going to do about my job and such. I always had the impression from day one that all they cared about was what they could get and how fast they could get it."

"Yeah, well, their plans backfired on them. Anyway, Marie is going to let the company in this afternoon so they can collect their furniture. After that, the place is yours to do as you please. I'll just need you to sign this document right here and these two documents when you're done." Dale pointed to show her the appropriate places to sign.

Clara signed on the dotted line a few times and began nodding her head in disbelief.

"What is it?" Dale asked.

"To think that I just moved out not too long ago. All that anxiety and stress. It was all for nothing. I never had to leave to begin with. Joan planned everything so nicely for me. This whole thing has been an absolute nightmare and quite frankly, I'm glad that it's over with," she said.

"I am, too. If you don't mind me asking, what caused you to change your mind? You seemed so adamant for a while. I was convinced you were about to give it all up."

"A few things, Dale. Joan's note played a major role. I felt like it gave me a chance to have one last conversation with her... to actually hear her wishes firsthand. Then, I'll blame the rest on me just needing time to process everything. This is a huge undertaking that I don't plan on taking lightly. I want to honor Joan's wishes to fill her place with all the joy and love that she once shared with her husband. I also want to be careful with the funds that she left and not squander it all. My folks didn't have much growing up. They busted their butts to make sure my sister and I had everything we needed growing up and then some. But, the one thing we both inherited from them was love. At first, I thought I couldn't honor my parents' legacy of love if I accepted the money and the house from Joan. How does the saying go? Money is the root of all evil? Mmm mmm," she grunted and took a deep breath.

"There's truth to that saying, Dale. I've seen how people can turn real ugly on you when they think money is involved. I've watched some of my loved ones act just as ugly as Olivia and her brother did. But, then it hit me. Joan was blessed to have everything that she's passed on and that never changed who she was at her core. She was loving, kind, giving, and a real friend. I can be all of those things, and I don't have to change who I am at the core. I can honor both of their legacies. My parents' and Joan's. That's why I changed my mind, Dale. That's why I can proudly sit here today and sign these papers," Clara said.

"Well, if time is what you needed, Clara, then I'm glad I was able to provide it for you. I deal with all types of cases, but it's rare that I come across stories like this. I'm happy for you and if you don't mind, I'd love for you to keep in touch and tell me how things are going. I know it sounds silly, but I'd love it if you'd shoot me an email every now and again to tell me how things are going with the house and all."

"Oh, Dale, Solomons Island is only but so big. I live in the café around the corner and I work at Lighthouse Tours. Do you know how easy it will be for me to pop in and say hello?" Clara said.

"That's wonderful. Yeah, I'm usually at the café on Tuesday evenings with my bowling team. I'm surprised I've never seen you in there before," Dale said.

Clara pointed toward herself.

"You're looking at the ultimate homebody who usually only comes out on Friday nights. But, now that I work across the street, I'm sure I'll be running into you more often," she said.

"Good."

CHAPTER 18

"*J*s this seat taken?" Mike asked.

Clara flipped her long red locks to the side. She was holding a milkshake in her hand while sipping from a straw when she paused and offered a welcoming smile.

"No, not at all. Long time no see, boss," she said jokingly, knowing he was aware she went to the café for lunch.

"Hey, I'm only your boss when we're on the clock, remember? Technically, lunch time doesn't count," he said.

Josh approached the two and asked if he could get Mike a menu.

"What's happening, buddy?" Mike said.

"Aww, you know, business as usual, I suppose. We're actually a little busier than usual with Mackenzie being out today," Josh said.

"Is she sick?" Mike asked.

"No, her daughter had a school play. She decided to take the day off and treat her daughter, too, after the play was over. You know Mack, she's just being an awesome mother as always," Josh said.

"Good for her. I know little Steph will remember times like this when she gets older."

"What are you having today?" Josh asked.

Mike glanced over at Clara's plate.

"I'll have whatever the lady is having, including the shake. Easy on the cherry," he said.

"One well done cheeseburger with fries and a vanilla milkshake coming right up." Josh marched to the kitchen with the order in hand.

Clara sat taking in the sound of dishes clanking in the back, the smell of good comfort food, and the view of Mike sitting beside her. She was committed to staying the course and keeping things professional, although secretly she had butterflies in her stomach every time he came near her.

"I can totally take my food to go if I'm imposing," he said.

"Oh, please. You're not bothering me one bit," she responded. Although, she knew that was a lie. She was highly distracted but determined to play it off.

"Cool. I actually wanted to get your opinion about something," Mike asked.

"Sure, what's up?"

"Two weeks from today is the sixth anniversary of Lighthouse Tours being in business. It also happens to be Ms. Mae's birthday. I was kind of hoping that we could partner up and plan a celebration gathering for the company but also combine it with a cake and recognition of her birthday. I was thinking we could even pull Jonathan in on the surprise so he could help us with Ms. Mae. What do you think?" he asked.

"I think that's a wonderful idea. Do have a place in mind to celebrate?"

"Not really, but that's where you would come in. It's going to include the folks from the Annapolis office as well. My partner and his wife are coming down, plus a couple of their employees. It would probably be best to go with a place that's quaint and intimate," Mike said.

"You mean, like the café? They have group events in here all the time. Plus, the location can't get any better than this. If you like the idea, I can talk to Mack and put the plans into motion as soon as she gets back," Clara offered.

"Why didn't I think of that? The café is perfect. We can celebrate with the team and present a cake to Ms. Mae. She won't even see it coming because she'll think we're here solely for our anniversary."

"Sounds like the perfect plan to me. I'll get on it first thing in the morning when Mack returns," Clara said.

"Perfect, thanks."

The conversation between Clara and Mike fell silent for a while. Talk of the celebration was replaced with the noise and hustle and bustle of the lunch crowd filing into the café. Josh delivered Mike's food to which he immediately dug into. Clara, on the other hand, was waiting for the perfect opportunity to address the pink elephant in the room.

"Hey, Mike," she said.

"Mm," he responded but tried not to open his mouth while he chewed.

"I'm sorry. Go ahead and finish your lunch. We can always talk at another time," she said.

"No, are you kidding me? Tell me what's on your mind."

She checked to make sure Josh was occupied and no one they knew was nearby.

"About this weekend. I don't even know how to say this, but... I hope we didn't make things awkward after, you know."

"I know exactly what you're trying to say, and I feel like I owe you an apology. The last thing I ever wanted to do was put you in an awkward employer vs employee situation. I genuinely felt like something was there between us, but that's beside the point. I was still wrong for acting on my feelings. I know I violated some sort of code of conduct law number one hundred and ninety-five, or something like it," he said.

Clara's laughter caused her to spray a bit of her milkshake on the counter. She quickly grabbed a napkin to clean it up and was totally embarrassed at her lack of control.

"Hold on a minute. I pour out the most genuine and sincere apology I can muster up and you laugh at me? What kind of nonsense is this?" Mike began laughing just as uncontrollably as Clara.

"It was law number one hundred and ninety-five that sent me over the edge. Sorry, but I couldn't help myself. Do you have all the codes and laws memorized?" she asked.

"No, wise guy. I'm just trying to show you that I'm really sorry and I'm a decent guy who knows how to conduct myself with employees. You just have a way about you...ugh, forget it. There I go again. Let me stop while I'm ahead," he said.

Clara patted her lips dry and looked up at Mike.

"I'm normally not that kind of woman. But, for whatever it's worth, I enjoyed spending the day with you."

The corner of Mike's mouth began to slowly rise as he tried to contain his smile.

"Likewise," he said. "As a matter of fact, I was kind of hoping you'd quit now that you're a wealthy woman and all," he teased.

Clara drew back and placed her hand on her hip.

"Excuse me? What happened to all the talk about me being valued and invited to work at Lighthouse Tours for as long as I please? I happen to like my job, you know," she said in her defense.

Clara was feeling somewhat playful and somewhat insulted all at the same time. If she was being honest with herself, she could pretend as if she was going to keep things professional all she wanted, but she liked Mike. The more they spent time together, the more obvious it was starting to become.

"And, I meant everything that I said about you. I promise, I will never tease like that again." He laughed.

"I sure hope not."

"Seriously, all jokes aside, can you keep a secret?" he asked.

"You won't meet a better secret keeper than me. Watcha got?"

"I haven't mentioned it to the team yet, but I plan on making a few more changes with the business in the near future. As soon as we get the new person on board and settled in, I want to start hunting for another location on the Island to open a charter division of the company," he said.

"Wow, that sounds exciting."

"Yeah, I was thinking that location would focus solely on boat rentals, fishing, maybe even a small fishing store attached. I just need to find the right space. It's definitely going to take some work organizing a new staff and gathering a new fleet of boats, but I think we can do it. The capital is there to get things up and running, I just need to find the right spot. I'll likely transition to the new location, especially for the initial start-up phase." Mike paused for a moment.

"Maybe that would help to create the healthy distance that we're so concerned about," Mike said.

Clara smiled while completely reading between the lines and thoroughly enjoying where he was going with it.

"Perhaps. How do you think the team will take the news? I mean, you guys have been working together forever, right?"

"Yes, but I think they'll be happy. They're aware that I've been looking for opportunities to expand outside of my partnership with my buddy, Kenny, so that part won't come as a surprise. I'll still share the Lighthouse Tours Annapolis location and this location across the street with him, but the Lighthouse charter division will be something I can call my own," he said proudly.

"Mike, in the short period of time I've been with the company, I can tell you definitely have what it takes to pull something like this off. I'm happy for you," Clara said.

"Thanks."

"So, what kind of time frame are you aiming for?" she asked.

"Six months, max. I'm ready to get this show on the road. Give or take a couple of months, depending on how the new employee works out. We'll have to see."

"Overseeing two places might become a handful if you don't plan this out carefully. Whatever you decide, you can count on me to help you stay organized," Clara promised.

"I appreciate that. I'm sure I'm going to need all the help I can get. In the meantime, I'd still like to continue our personal tour, Clara. I think it would be beneficial for you to learn as much as you can about the area while I still have time. I promise not to misbehave. Maybe we can even invite Mack and her daughter Stephanie on the next tour to be our chaperones."

"I'd like to think we can handle ourselves," she said.

"Speak for yourself." He stopped to look around and then looked directly into Clara's eyes.

"You're smart, you're beautiful, and you have such a humble spirit. Any guy will kill to be with somebody like you, Clara. The sooner I can find the location for the new division and be on my way, the better off we'll both be."

"And, until then?" she asked.

"I'm going to do the right thing and be the gentleman and professional that I'm supposed to be. Even if it goes against everything we're feeling right now, I think it's best. You deserve that amount of respect from me," he said.

Although Clara felt a slight bit of disappointment settling

in, she knew it was the right thing to do. She barely recognized this new desire for thrill and romance, but she knew that now was not the time and perhaps Mike was not the right guy.

"Mike, I promise this will be the last unprofessional question that I ask you, but you talk about all my qualities and how any guy would kill to be with me. What about you? How come you're not with someone special?" Clara asked.

Mike poked his straw around in his shake and stirred it a bit before responding.

"I was engaged once. She was the love of my life. She was kind, compassionate, and believe it or not, a red head just like yourself." He sniggled.

"We both served in the Coast Guard together. There were just three weeks left until our wedding day before the accident happened. An explosion broke out below the main deck that left her and two others trapped. They were out at sea, and while the others tried to do all they could to save their lives, she didn't make it."

"Oh my God," Clara said.

"Yep, it was a difficult pill to swallow. I didn't exactly do a good job of handling the news back then. I left the military shortly after. It was a rough road for a while, and I guess you could say, I haven't found anyone to truly love ever since."

"Man. How long ago did this happen?" she asked.

"This summer marks ten years since she's been gone."

"I'm so sorry, Mike," she said with emotion.

Clara felt sorry for bringing it up, yet happy that he appeared to be at a much stronger place in his life. It reminded her that the old saying was true, you never know what a man's been through until you've walked a mile in his shoes.

CHAPTER 19

$\mathcal{M}$s. Mae's house was filled with all the things that made her heart sing. Her grandchildren were running around in the backyard giggling and having a good time, her daughter, Lily, was helping her set the table for lunch, and Jonathan was helping Mae's son-in-law replace a rotting bush out front.

"Mom, you've been awfully cheerful since we arrived. I know you're happy to see the kids and all, but is something going on that I'm not aware of?" Lily asked.

"What do you mean? Can't I just be happy to see you without any strings attached?"

"Yeah, but you're extra happy. I mean, really happy," Lily emphasized.

"Again, what's wrong with being happy? Am I missing something here?"

"Okay, I didn't think I needed to spell it out like this, but you're glowing." Lily checked over her shoulder.

"That kind of glow can only be found when you've been with a man," Lily whispered.

Ms. Mae immediately felt exposed.

"Oh, dear, is it that obvious?"

"I knew it! You and Jonathan are a hot item now, aren't you?" Lily asked.

Ms. Mae placed her vegetables on the chopping board and put her knife down.

"Lily, there you go being nosey. You are just like your mother!" Ms. Mae said with a smile.

Lily burst out in laughter. She did grow up to be just like Ms. Mae in many ways and apparently being nosey was another inherited trait to add to the list.

"You still have me beat when it comes to poking your nose around," Lily said.

Ms. Mae had a smirk on her face knowing full well that her daughter was right. She loved to live vicariously through Lily and had a way about prying and poking around when she was curious about her personal life.

"Well, am I right?" Lily asked.

"Yes, we're an item now. We were going to sit you down and share the news together, but I guess you beat me to it," Ms. Mae said.

"Hey, there's no need for formalities with me. Besides, it's about time you two made it official. Actually, the time is long overdue. Steven and the kids and I love Jonathan. He's always been such a great friend to you."

"It makes me feel good to hear you say that, Lily. I've always wondered how you'd feel about me moving on after your father's passing. I guess I never could find the right words to bring it up, so I didn't address it at all. It's pretty silly now that I think about it," Ms. Mae confessed.

"It's been a long time, Mom. I can see you wanting to keep his memory alive, but even I would hope that you wouldn't blow an opportunity to be with a good man who adores you the way Jonathan does," Lily said.

Ms. Mae tried to compose herself, but a floodgate of tears let loose. It was almost as if she'd been quietly waiting for permission to move on all these years. Ms. Mae released the buildup of emotions, and Lily comforted her as best as she knew how.

In the midst of hugging, the men walked in from out front. With their shirts drenched in sweat and dirty knees, they stood in bewilderment staring at the two emotional women.

"We go outside for two minutes to dig out a bad bush and come back in here to find you crying. What's the matter with you, Mae? Are the onions getting to you, or is it something else?" Jonathan asked.

Steven chimed in, "Are y'all all right?"

"We're fine. We were just having a mother and daughter moment, that's all. Now, may I ask why you two are tracking all that dirt into my house?" Ms. Mae asked as she stood with her hands on her hips inspecting the floor. It was her crafty way of changing the subject for now. Later on, she still had intentions of talking things over with everyone, including Jonathan.

"I'll go get the broom, but the two of you might want to step outside with Jonathan. We have a little surprise that we think you'll enjoy," Steven said.

Outside, Ms. Mae and Lily were delighted by the replacement bush. But, to the left of it was an additional bush with a plaque dedicated as a memorial to their late husband and father. Ms. Mae read the plaque repeatedly and was in awe of the kind gesture. It was those acts of kindness that reminded Ms. Mae that Jonathan was everything she needed and wanted in a man. He was perfect for her in every way.

∼

Clara sat on the edge of the dock behind her home. At first, she glanced at her footprints in the sand and then she looked toward the house. She still struggled with the reality that it all belonged to her, but with every day that passed, it was slowly starting to sink in. Thankfully, a couple of weeks had passed and she hadn't heard any more from Olivia and her brother. Things were finally starting to settle down again, and she couldn't be more pleased with her new reality.

Back at the house she could hear Holly barking uncontrollably. It was the distinct sound she made to signal that someone was at the front door.

"Hold on, Holly. It sure would be nice if you could ignore the door so your momma can take in some sun," Clara said as she hurried to return to the house.

Once inside she brushed the sand off her feet, put on some shoes, and proceeded to calm Holly down.

"Holly, hush. It's okay, girl. I'll get the door, it's okay," she said.

She checked the app on her cell connected to the front camera. The wide angle revealed an image of Mike turning around and walking toward his jeep.

"Mike?" she said.

He turned around with an emerging smile.

"Hey, I was beginning to think I had the wrong place," he said.

"No, you have the right place. I was just out back taking in the sun. If it wasn't for Holly, I wouldn't have known anyone was here."

Holly danced around Mike's feet and sniffed him ferociously with a wagging tail. It was nothing that Mike couldn't settle down with a few strokes and a little attention.

"I didn't mean to interrupt you. I just happened to be in the area heading to the office. I remembered you saying something about your new place being close to the beach. I didn't realize you were this close. This is amazing," he said.

"Yeah, Joan had a thing for beachfront properties. I got pretty lucky, I guess."

She continued to watch him play with Holly.

"Would you like to come in?" Clara asked.

He hesitated for a moment.

"Well, again, I don't want to disturb you. It was probably dumb of me to pop in unannounced," Mike said.

"I don't mind. It's just me in this big old place. Sometimes it's nice to have a little company."

"I can imagine." He stood awkwardly and ran his fingers through his hair.

"For a minute there, I thought you were going to tell me you were here for another personal tour," she said.

"How about that. We did have a nice time on our last tour, didn't we?" he asked.

By now Clara suspected something was up. Mike appeared to have more on his mind than he was letting on, and even seemed a bit nervous.

"Hey, by the way, I just want to thank you again for putting on a phenomenal party for our sixth anniversary. You and Mackenzie really pulled it together. Ms. Mae was totally surprised, and I still keep receiving positive feedback from the crew over at the Annapolis office about how much they enjoyed everything," he said.

"It was my pleasure. I had a blast, myself. It was nice getting a chance to meet everybody."

"Yeah, you really seemed to hit it off with my partner's wife, Ann. Hopefully, this won't be the last time you two get together," Mike said.

"Oh, I agree. She was so sweet."

Mike stood there for another minute before backing away

slowly to his car. Then, he stopped completely and locked eyes with Clara.

"Clara, I need to be upfront with you while I still have the nerve," he said.

"What's wrong?" she asked.

"Nothing other than I'm not being completely honest with myself or with you. It's been two weeks since we sat in the café and had that heart-to-heart conversation. I'm sure you remember it well. I told you I wanted to do things the right way and be a professional. I told you I wanted to at least wait until I moved to the new location, remember?"

"Yes," she said.

"I've tried really hard since that day to push you out of my mind. I've avoided late evenings with you, too much interaction in the office, eating at the café with you, I've kept it strictly business. But, there's only one problem. I can't get you out of my mind. I can't stop thinking about you. I loved being there for you that night you were afraid and needed somebody by your side. I loved taking the tours with you. And, the kiss. I can't stop thing about kissing you not once but multiple times and it feeling so right. I can't even stop thinking about the first night we met. I didn't give a damn about the headlamp then, and I still don't now. I was intrigued by you. You captivated my attention with your beauty and your sassy fire as you marched over to my car," Mike said.

Clara chuckled. "I was hot and ready to tell you a thing or two," she said.

"You sure were." Mike walked closer until the only thing between them was the threshold of her front door.

"God knows I never expected that you'd come and work for me, Clara. I never expected you to follow through. But, once you walked through that door, there was no way I could let you go. I'm starting to believe we crossed paths for reasons deeper than we originally knew," he said.

Clara's heart was racing to the point where she wondered if he could hear it out loud. She could feel Mike's breath as he spoke. She felt like she was in a trance and didn't know what to say.

"I have good news," he said

"What is it?" she whispered.

"It's still early yet, but I think I may have a couple of locations in mind for the new division."

"Is that your way of telling me you may be leaving the current office even earlier than you anticipated?" Clara asked.

"Something like that. It's still going to take a lot of moving parts to make it happen. Plus, I have to start hunting for the new hire. But, I was hoping you'd be willing to help me with the process."

"Of course," she said.

It was all Clara could do to control her desire to reach out and touch Mike.

"And, what about us?" she asked.

"The way I see it, we get to make our own rules. Just like Ms. Mae and Jonathan did. They're the ultimate professionals. Nothing gets in the way of their work. They both do a great job for the company, but they also don't allow anything to get in the way of their love for each other."

Mike gently kissed her bottom lip and then stopped as if he were seeking permission to continue.

"Hold me and kiss me," she whispered.

Mike dove in for a full-fledged kiss. That afternoon, he left her with a taste of something new and invigorating. Something she hadn't experienced in a very long time. He ignited a flame in her and gave her the desire to love.

Ready for book two of the Solomons Island series?

She's forty-eight, single, and falling head over heels for Mike, her new boss.

He's equally intrigued, but will circumstances deem their love to be permissible or forbidden?

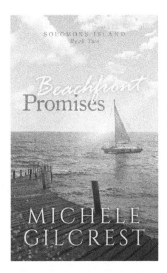

In book two of the Solomons Island series Clara is ready to move forward from her year of loss and pain, and she's ready to ignite a new flame. However, she may find herself faced with a few stumbling blocks along the way.

As luck would have it, there's a secret from Clara's past that manages to resurface at the most inconvenient time. If not handled carefully this secret could cost her inheritance, and another chance at love.

Then, there's the question of maintaining a certain level of professionalism while falling completely, deeply, and hopelessly in love with her boss, Mike Sanders.

Will Clara overcome these significant challenges to finally experience her happily ever after?

The story wouldn't be complete without checking in with the other employees who work alongside Clara at the Lighthouse company. The continuation of Ms. Mae's love story is sure to give you butterflies as she turns up the heat with her longtime friend, and now lover, Jonathan.

Pull up a beach chair and enjoy book two of the Solomons Island series – a sweet, romantic beach read!

<u>Looking for another beach read? Check out the Pelican Beach series!</u>

She's recently divorced. He's a widower. Will a chance encounter lead to true love?

If you like sweet romance about second chances then you'll love The Inn At Pelican Beach!

At the Inn, life is filled with the unexpected.

Payton is left to pick up the pieces after her divorce is finalized. Seeking a fresh start, she returns to her home town in Pelican Beach.

Determined to move on with her life, she finds herself caught up in the family business at The Inn. It may not be her passion, but anything is better than what her broken marriage had to offer.

Payton doesn't wallow in her sorrows long before her opportunity at a second chance shows up. Is there room in her heart to love again? She'll soon find out!

In this first book of the Pelican Beach series, passion, renewed strength, and even a little sibling rivalry are just a few of the emotions that come to mind.

Visit The Inn and walk hand in hand with Payton as she heals and seeks to restore true love.

Get your copy of this clean romantic beach read today!

<u>Pelican Beach Series-</u>

The Inn At Pelican Beach: Book 1

Sunsets At Pelican Beach: Book 2

A Pelican Beach Affair: Book 3

Christmas At Pelican Beach: Book 4

Sunrise At Pelican Beach: Book 5

CPSIA information can be obtained
at www.ICGtesting.com
Printed in the USA
LVHW080212180621
690358LV00022B/3104

9 781953 722089